Hisland

SUNY Series, The Margins of Literature

Mihai I. Spariosu, Editor

Hisland

Adventures in Ac-Ac-ademe

Fedwa Malti-Douglas

State University of New York Press

Illustration by Slim, 1996.

The characters and events in this work are fictitious. Any resemblance to actual persons or events is purely coincidental.

Published by
State University of New York Press, Albany

For information, address State University of New York Press,
State University Plaza, Albany, N.Y. 12246

Production by M. R. Mulholland
Marketing by Fran Keneston

Library of Congress Cataloging-in-Publication Data

Malti-Douglas, Fedwa.
    Hisland : adventures in ac-ac-ademe / Fedwa Malti-Douglas.
        p.   cm. — (SUNY series, the margins of literature)
    ISBN 0-7914-3603-9 (HC : acid free).

    I. Title. II. Series.
    PS3563.A4336H57 1997
    813'.54—dc21   97-1207
                                                                              CIP

10 9 8 7 6 5 4 3 2 1

Contents

Introduction

A bomb? That was what ran through my mind as I opened my office door that day and looked at the box lying on my desk. Plain brown paper. No return address. A typed mailing label with my name spelled correctly (not a given, I should add) and my Women's Studies address. Never mind. My part-time appointment in Women's Studies meant that I received much of my mail there and not in the department I chaired. (Why we in Women's Studies are mostly made of parts I will never understand but it is certainly a point worth thinking about.)

I was intrigued. My secretary (one of the privileges of being a lowly administrator) was watching me. I could tell she was also wondering what this was about. Lest she (and I of course) die of curiosity, I proceeded to open the package. It was a box, the kind in which university letterhead paper arrives. I opened the box and was greeted by a bound volume with a letter clipped to it.

I read:

> My dearest Female Fellow Traveler in Academe,
>
> I have long been an admirer of your books on women. You may even notice that I have been inspired by your work. [*Not a bad beginning, I thought!*]
>
> Forgive my impudence in sending you this manuscript. If you are at all like me (that's even more of an impudent thought), I know you will read the enclosed text. [*Who is this person, I thought, who seems to know me better than I know myself?*]
>
> Now for the outrageous part. I am sending you the novel as a present. It would honor me greatly if you would write an introduction to the novel and publish it.
>
> I do not care if it appears under my name. [*That's a first, I thought!*] It is more important to me that *Ac-Ac*, for that is the title of the novel, see the light of day. In fact, I would much prefer that you attach your name to it and publish it wherever you deem fit.
>
> I lived the experience of Ac-Ac and attempted to exorcise it in words. Forgive me if I bequeath you the burden of carrying those words into print.
>
> With gratitude.
> M/M.

M/M. What an odd name, I thought. And why would such a person send me a volume to read and introduce? I looked once again at the package. I had not noticed before that the post office had left its own indelible mark on it: a slip of official government paper indicating that the package had been damaged in shipment and rewrapped by one of Uncle Sam's lackeys. My name and address, the government form added, had been transferred to the newly rewrapped package, but unfortunately the name and address of the sender had forever disappeared. Great! This certainly was a bomb, but not the kind I had initially thought.

Write an introduction to a novel whose author was reduced to initials? Even more strange, write an introduction to a novel by an author who is not only willing to give up authorship of her novel (I somehow knew that M/M was a woman) but would rather not even play the authorship game so beloved to academics? And what kind of responsibility was this placing on my already-weary shoulders?

A bomb, indeed. I sat down at my desk, asked my secretary to close my office door, and entered the world of *Ac-Ac*. Within a minute, I had answered my own question: the introduction would be forthcoming, but not exactly as M/M had foreseen. Most of it would come after the novel: a postduction or afterword (that would be fashionably postmodern anyway). And M/M, whoever and wherever she was, would, I was sure, somehow understand this.

—Fedwa Malti-Douglas

Ac-Ac

Acknowledgments

Thanks go:
for inspiration, to my colleagues;
for unswerving support, to my bra.

Dedication

(This Space for Rent)

In Which M/M Lands on Her Feet

The hot air balloon crashes. What a richly ironic event! I have just been promoted to full professor (or is it fool professor?). After ten years at the big Pholly U., I, M/M, have just passed my last academic exam. I am the first woman to achieve that exalted status in my department. Ned Thornwipple, the one chaired professor in the department, prepared my dossier for the dean's committee. It seemed appropriate that the only present I could offer myself was a ride in a hot air balloon. I could not do it in December when the promotion decisions were announced. No matter. It is now June and the weather is perfect for this outing. After all, I had survived ten years surrounded by hot air, why not go up in it for a change? The hot air balloon crashes on a beach area. I walk away unscathed. My cat of two years, S. P.-T., accompanies me.

This is definitely a possible beginning. But, let us try another one. I, M/M, have just completed my Ph.D. from Pholly University. Sounds final, doesn't it? Great thesis, my advisor, Professor Ned Thornwipple, tells me. "Reading as a Marxist, Masturbating as a Woman" was the title I finally settled on. And that was after much mental (and need I add physical) masturbation. How that old twit Thornwipple could like this work remains a mystery to me. Thank God that is all over.

"M/M, you should think twice about being a scholar," he would tell me, sounding solicitous.

"M/M, you should be a librarian."

Why my future seemed so crucial to him I am beginning to understand only now. Here it is June and all that is ahead of me at this point is a summer of relaxation before I officially turn into that unpredictable creature, an Assistant Professor in the English department at Pholly. True, the university administration had sent out a very eloquent memo asking departments to refrain from hiring their own students. But a little incest never hurts, does it? Before beginning the drudgery, I decide to offer myself a little vacation: a solitary cruise on a private yacht. No one knows my secret fantasy: living in an enormous house boat, with plenty of room for my library. Anchored in a marina but yet able to drift if the mood hits me. Could anything be more perfect? I guess I will settle now for a nice private cruise that will mentally prepare me for the new semester. The only being that I will permit to share my days and nights on this cruise is my cat of two years, S. P.-T.

These might have been the opening paragraphs of a nice autobiographical account by yours truly, M/M, either at the beginning of a possibly optimistic career or after ten years of a grueling academic life.

But no. Not because this is not all true. Nor because I did not go either on the cruise or up in the hot air balloon. No. Simply because it is now a year later and I have swallowed my adventure on the Islands of Ac-Ac. And what a stomach ache I have from this indigestible meal! If I do not vomit it, it will kill me. If it were to kill me, I would be simply a murder victim in yet another academic novel written by yet another woman academic. Of all the luck in the world. Why could not I have been born a man? Then I might have landed in an academic novel written by a male academic. There, there are no murders. My life would be but a series of love affairs, a series of sycophantic students. Hopping from international conference to international conference. I would be seducing my colleagues' wives. I would become the chairman (note the "man"—so beloved to authority figures—at the end of that word) of my department. My dream of becoming a dean and eventually a provost, and who knows even a university president, might have a chance of becoming a reality. But my literary physical plumbing has doomed me. Do not misunderstand me: I am at least grateful not to be in a murder novel.

Why me? Why the crash? Why the storm that comes up as soon as I set sail? Ah, were it not for these freak events, where would I be? Yet another professor sleepwalking through the myriad duties of a university life. My education would be lacking. But here I am alone after the accident.

This close call decides it once and for all: I prefer to be M/M the full professor. I do not believe in revenants and, let us face it, after my ten years at Pholly U., how can I pretend to be that innocent creature I might have once been?

In Which M/M Arrives at Ac-Ac U.

I should have smelled something wrong when I spotted the old figure walking on the beach. An apparition from comic strips: a skinny male with a beard, sporting a top hat, wearing a black suit. He is followed by a coterie of males, all with the same black suit, all wearing wire-rimmed glasses, all sputtering phrases I could not understand.

Virtual statues, they stand staring at me. I am wearing jeans and a Pholly U. sweatshirt. A far cry from their clothing. My short hair (I had just had it cut for the summer) is hidden under a hat.

The old man addresses me:

"I am Professor Hoodwinkle. Who are you?"

My God. My first reaction is to burst out in laughter. Thornwipple—Hoodwinkle. Are these two cousins? I thought I had escaped that web. But restraining myself, I do not laugh.

"I am M/M," I hear myself saying.

"M period M period?" he asks.

"No. M slash M."

His face begins to change color.

"A woman," he gasps.

Yes, I am a woman. And, what of it, I am tempted to say. But Mind your Manners M/M.

"Is there a problem with that?" my voice responds of its own free will.

"No. No. Not at all," the old man replies.

But his words express one thing, his face, another.

Come to find out, I had landed on the Islands of Ac-Ac. Yes, you are about to ask me. Where the hell are those islands and why have not the United States Navy, Army, Air Force, and Marines (not to speak of all those other good guys) heard of them? The world is full of mysterious places and this is certainly one of them. I had lost myself a bit during the trip—lofty thoughts of academe—and so had no inkling of how far I had gone. I must admit that Hoodwinkle's appearance took me by surprise.

In Which M/M Gets Her Bearings

Professor Hoodwinkle (he does not like being called by any other name) is more than generous and hospitable, offering to give me a tour of the Islands. He warms up to me because of my shocking pink Pholly U. sweatshirt. It seems that the reputation of this august institution has preceded it, even to the Islands of Ac-Ac. Wanting to appear friendly, I ask him if he knows Ned Thornwipple.

"Ah, yes," comes the answer. "I have had occasion to read some of his works."

I try not to laugh. Thornwipple was known around the department for being an old fart and his scholarly ideas were by now undatable, unless you wanted to subject his brain to carbon dating. Oh, never mind. He was still debating whether the main character of Irving Goosebump's novel was a hero or an anti-hero. In his first major article, he tried to prove that he was a hero. In a later major article, he proved himself wrong, arguing for the anti-hero thesis.

"So, how is old Thornwipple?" is the next question.

Just fine, just fine. I hesitate. Do I tell Hoodwinkle, sorry Professor Hoodwinkle, about poor Ned's latest adventures? He was caught in the ladies' room of the English department. What old Ned was doing there is still a mystery. He claims he wandered in by mistake.

"Oh, little old absent-minded me," he kept repeating, trying to convince anyone who would listen.

But the freshman (oops, excuse me), I mean the first-year student, who caught him peeping at her through the hole of the next cubicle had other—and less savory—things to say. Here we were all sure that Thornwipple was gay, but he proved us wrong. Word had it that he liked to hang around one of the men's rooms in the administration building where it was rumored that young men would stand around and masturbate for anyone who cared to watch. Ah! Good old Thornwipple. Those were mere rumors.

I had been privileged to become the confidante of a female graduate student in the department just as Thornwipple had been promoted to the role of graduate advisor. There she was in his office for a necessary signature. And there he was in his swivel chair, moving closer and closer to her. He began slowly enough, commenting on her physical beauty. But no sooner had he finished his comments than his right hand had already wound its way down to his crotch. Thornwipple had the good taste not to whip out his penis. He restricted himself to stroking his organ through his clothing. The graduate student ran out of the room. Disgusting and unprofessional behavior, which the student did not wish to make public. Now you see why I chose my title: "Reading as a Marxist, Masturbating as a Woman?" Give Thornwipple a thorn or two.

P. (I decide to call him that for short) Hoodwinkle is not really listening to the answer anyway. He is more anxious to make sure that I learn what he can teach me about the Islands. Ac-Ac has a long history, it turns out. The only thing I remember of his tour is that this had been a wildlife preserve (might a zoo be more appropriate here I think?) until Ac-Ac U. was founded on it. P.H. (I was in favor of more shortening!) was the first professor hired to teach and he filled the institution (the right word for it!) in his own image. And what an image, I would learn. Having been brought up to be a good listener, I let P.H. drone on, something he takes for encouragement. How surprised I then was by his invitation to spend a semester, or as much time as I liked, in his and his colleagues' august company and learn as much as I wanted about Ac-Ac U.

Instead of the gold-embossed invite, I got:

"We have a top-notch university here. We are always striving for excellence. Oh, and stop me before I sing the praises of all our departments."

Oh, do, do stop, P.H.

"We have a most excellent language department with fine, fine faculty."

"Sounds great to me," I assured P.H., and off we went.

In Which M/M Wonders:
Why Be a Visiting Professor at Ac-Ac U. When She Could Be at Pholly U.?

I think this topic has to be discussed. My years at Pholly U. had certainly been interesting ones. But it never hurts to add a little distinction to one's curriculum vitae, does it? I had noticed that my c.v. lacked a little sparkle in the area of concurrent positions. A Visiting Professor at Ac-Ac U. is not as prestigious as the Revolving Chair at Pholly U. but no one has offered me that yet.

P.H. was a convincing salesperson. This would be the perfect moment to be visiting the U. The semester was not yet in full swing. Faculty were busy preparing their syllabi and annual reports. The deans were getting ready for the one university-wide faculty meeting of the year, which I was assured everyone would attend. There would be promotion dossiers to prepare, positions to fill. Memos would flow like wine. I would have access to all this material and more, all in the name of science, of course. What more could my heart desire?

I still hesitated. What impression could I have simply by being around a college, not really part of any department, flitting from one meeting to another? P.H. had the perfect solution. Why not, he suggested, simply choose one department to settle in, the department of my choice! Indeed, the perfect solution. The only question remaining was: which department? P.H. volunteered to fill me in briefly on some of the more distinguished departments.

In Which M/M Gets a Lecture on Academic Hierarchies

I could tell that P.H. felt uncomfortable with my name.

"Just M/M, huh?," he would repeatedly and emphatically ask.

"Yes," I would just as repeatedly and just as emphatically answer.

"No Professor or Dr. before it?"

"No."

By now, P.H. had accepted, albeit not too gracefully, my status as full professor at the institution he so much admired. He had also sent one of his minions to the library to look me up and sure enough my books showed up on the data banks. So I was a bona fide person.

But no title? That really seemed to bother him.

"You know, M/M, our fine university thrives on titles. How else would we spot the professors from the mere hangers-on? No institution can exist without hierarchy. What else would our colleagues have to live for if they did not have that?"

Poor P.H. His mouth was twitching. He could barely get the words out.

"I am sorry, *Professor* Hoodwinkle."

I was sure to put the emphasis on Professor.

"M/M it will be."

"As you wish, M/M."

He grudgingly gave in. Not only was I challenging the hierarchy but I was challenging his authority. This test of wills was important for me. He promised me he would make sure his colleagues addressed me as I wished to be addressed.

In Which M/M Has a Second Landing at Ac-Ac: A Home Department

P.H.'s voice had that quality that invariably puts a listener to sleep. Sitting in his office and listening to him drone on, my ears would perk up only now and then. The incident reminded me of the heartless—yet funny—way a Pholly U. student had summed up one of my colleagues on an evaluation form: "Dr. X. makes Sominex seem like speed." These words will follow the hapless Dr. X. to her dying day (yes, Dr. X. is a she!): they had been published in the yearly student publication, *Pholly's Follies*. At the time, I felt sorry for my colleague. Now, facing Hoodwinkle, my feelings went out to the student.

It took a great deal of effort on my part to concentrate on his monotone. How does one choose an academic home on the spot? I had not, after all, met any of my would-be colleagues. But I felt sure that whatever choice I made would not have serious consequences. This was not a permanent position. I was not being placed in an academic marriage from which there would be no escape. Academic divorce was unheard of at Pholly U. where tenure was a marriage "in sickness or in health," mental that is. Mental health was the less likely outcome. My ten years had convinced me that the life of the mind was not a desideratum in academia. Would Ac-Ac U. be different, I wondered?

I noticed much to my surprise that the only two departments at Ac-Ac U. that held any interest for me whatsoever were the Department of Past, Present, and Future Events and that of Unusual Languages and Literatures. I tried to stop P.H.'s droning and get him to fill in more details for me.

"Well, M/M," he started out, "the Department of Past, Present, and Future Events might be a great choice."

It turned out that for this group, the Past was sort of a blur. The Present was here and now and for every one in the department that was unquestionably M/M.

"What? Me?"

"Yes," P.H. was quick to answer. "You, young lady," (it took all my control not to slap him across the room—I hated that phrase) "have become a full-time occupation for that fine department."

I love being turned into an occupation. But let us give this a chance, I decided. It turned out those wonderful members of that department had found me incredibly fascinating. What was I doing there? How could a woman travel alone? Why was I wearing pants on arrival? One faculty member who had a crystal ball in his office claimed he had predicted my arrival. He had seen a speck on the ball one day. And there I was! This distinguished researcher had spent time among coffee drinkers and tea drinkers in various parts of the world and could read coffee cups. His preferred "text" was thick coffee whose sediments stuck in the cup. He absolutely hated it when people came to him and asked him to read their cups of decaffeinated coffee.

He would tell them: "You don't understand, decaf is very watery. It will not hold a shape even if you make espresso out of it."

But in this health-conscious age, he could do nothing but give in to people's decaf urge. So he did his best and, of course, everyone became angry when he made predictions from decaf whose opposite became true.

I thought long and hard as P.H. was selling this masterful academic group. To be an object of fascination was not my goal in life. I could not possibly expect to function for an entire semester with individuals who could not see me as one of them. After all, how could a speck on a crystal ball ever come close to a professor in that department? That took care of the Department of Past, Present, and Future Events.

"What about Unusual Languages and Literatures," I heard myself asking.

"Ah, young lady," (*Christ, will he ever stop with that?*) "you will never regret that decision. The Department of Unusual Languages and Literatures: and mind you we do not normally refer to it with the word Department before the title. The acronym would not properly reflect the high esteem in which we hold our dear colleagues there."

(*DULL? It can't be!*) Letters had always been magical to me and, to be frank, the acronym decided it: DULL it would be!

In Which M/M Describes Her Third Landing of Sorts

How could I forget to talk about my material life? This DULL business was making me absent-minded! Well, come to discover, non-human companions were unknown at Ac-Ac. Cats were considered by these high-minded intellectuals not to be worthy of human attention. That did it for me. I tried not to vomit as P.H. was explaining this. What did he want me to do? Get rid of S. P.-T.? Not on your life! I tried to explain but finally gave up. S. P.-T. was not a pet. So what if she was a Maine Coon? That was irrelevant. To me, she was a real person. I would rather see this human standing before me disappear. Sure, I was a misanthrope. I had been accused of that before. Not an accusation as far as I was concerned. A compliment, rather. This attitude to what to me were higher creatures took care of any positive sentiments I might ever have for the Ac-Acians. I stood firm. Even this thick-skulled creation could see that.

So what could Ac-Ac U. do? The president, with P.H.'s intervention, graciously offered me a room at the University Guest House for the length of my visit. Great honor, etc. Yes, I knew all about these things. Residence in the Guest House also gave me access to the Faculty Club. The practical side of this? I did not have to cook, something I hate anyway. I did not have to clean my room. My everyday necessities would be taken care of and I could concentrate my energies on learning all there was to learn about Ac-Ac. I even received presidential permission to keep S. P.-T. with me in the Guest House. I did not have to do without my true friend, someone who had shared many of my woes and joys. Take me, take her. That had been my bottom line.

Poor P.H. This must have been one of his most difficult tasks. But he accomplished it. S. P.-T. would be there to greet me as I walked into the suite. Hah! She and I also had a good laugh. How often had she heard me fume about my aversion to faculty clubs as strongholds of male power? This was the height of irony. A double Hah!

The only problem with the Guest House was its absence of books. Rather odd for an academic institution. My house back at Pholly U. was overrun with books. S. P.-T. was a real book cat. Whenever a new shipment of books came into the house, she would be all over them, climbing, sniffing, chewing, trying to literally consume all the material. I had awarded her a MacCatArthur Award for her high intelligence and inquisitive mind. I certainly could not have written my books without her. What would she do at the Guest House? I was hoping she would take comfort in the plethora of memos that I somehow guessed Ac-Ac U. would be wonderful at producing.

In Which M/M Gets Her First Introduction to DULL

I asked P.H. if he could first arrange for me to meet with the Chair of the Department of Unusual Languages and Literatures so I could be assured of his total cooperation.

"Certainly," my guide was quick to respond. "Any chairman would be honored to have you, the great M/M, as a visitor for the semester. There is only one problem, however. I understand that the current chairman is being replaced with a new one so why not meet both?"

"Terrific idea," I was just as quick to respond.

The outgoing chair of DULL! Could he have been chosen better? I doubted it! Professor Ubris Hirsute-du-Vigneron. Short and undistinguished looking with his back hunched over. The buttons on his rumpled shirt seemed on the edge of popping, barely able to contain his protruding beer belly. Part of the shirt had managed to escape from the belt's confines and hung limply over the pants. He smiled at me and seemed friendly enough. I was assured of his full cooperation and he took it upon himself to tell me that he could speak for the entirety of the department when he welcomed me in the warmest possible way. He had chaired the department for many years and volunteered to fill me in on its history. Meanwhile, how about some material to take home and look at?

I hesitated. Reading the department files, newsletters, and minutes was a wonderful idea. It would provide me with important insights. I was still uneasy. I conveyed my hesitations to P.H. The cooperation of the outgoing chair was very important. But what about the newly appointed chair? P.H. himself had suggested that I meet him. Professor Ubris Hirsute-du-Vigneron was listening to the exchange between me and my academic guide. The problem was that Professor Assam was not in the office yet. When would he arrive? Shortly. P.H.

and I decided, simultaneously it seemed, that we would be happy to wait for him. Anxious to get his name right, I asked Hirsute-du-Vigneron to spell it out for me.

"Just like the tea," he assured me.

Pleased with his rhetorical abilities, he then asked P.H. and me if we would like some of the brew. Since waiting was in the cards, we both graciously accepted. I took the occasion to walk around the central office of DULL. Travel posters papered the walls. Exotic places are around the corner, they seemed to be saying, if only you sign up for our courses. Pictures of smiling rotund male faculty greeted the student. This boded well for my visit.

No sooner had we settled in to drink our tea than we became aware of a great commotion. The computer keyboards began humming. The printers began buzzing. Intermingled voices indicated that the boss had just arrived. Following P.H.'s signal, I got up in anticipation of the great moment. Professor Assam was already in his office, having entered it by a back door. This I would come to learn was part and parcel of the game of power. Private entrances that allow one to appear and disappear like some supernatural being. More important than the private entrances were the private bathrooms. Ah. Lucky was the chair who was privy to a privy for his future was assured. A private bathroom was the public sign of true departmental support on the part of Ac-Ac U.'s administration.

Professor Hirsute-du-Vigneron's numerous knocks on the door of Chair Assam's office produced no results. He looked embarrassed but undaunted. He disappeared for a few minutes and reappeared on the other side of the door leading to the sacred space. He ushered us in with great gusto and we were met by a tall, gray-haired, grave-looking individual who was introduced to us as Professor Assam.

I must say I had trouble containing my shock when I heard P.H.'s voice announcing his pleasure and excitement at meeting this extraordinary colleague about whom he had heard so much.

Extraordinary? P.H. had been quite free with the word "distinguished." No, gentlemen, let us be honest here. It was not only P.H. who took liberties with this poor overused word. It seemed to be the word of the month, if not the year, at Ac-Ac U. But "extraordinary?" This was truly a descriptive worth watching. I would have liked to have scratched my head on that one, preferably like my darling S. P.-T. with her rear paw, but I had not yet mastered that technique. So I simply stood, I am sure looking quite ridiculous, with my mouth open.

P.H. nudged me and I watched my arm extend itself—of its free will it seemed—to shake hands with this creature. I muttered some nice words. Trained to be polite, that is what I was. Professor Assam garbled some words back and motioned us to sit down.

His was a most luxurious office with a rectangular table on one side surrounded by chairs. As I would learn, this was for private meetings with faculty and with the Departmental Council. P.H. and I had the good fortune to be motioned to the only comfortable-looking place in the room, a couch placed against the wall. Assam sat in his tall chair behind his desk and Hirsute-du-Vigneron was opposite P.H. and me. I felt the two of us were on show.

It took me a moment to realize that Professor Assam was addressing me. His words were difficult to understand. I could not ask P.H. what was going on. So I let him do the talking. Something he seemed to be more than happy doing. I had learned to tune myself out for these perorations. And well I might, for they were usually about me. I had also learned to plaster a nice smile on my face while I supposedly listened to these male voices. Smiles were beginning to appear on the faces of the others as they stared at me. This was usually my cue that the perorations were about to end and that I could begin to half listen. Sure enough, it was the usual assurances of welcome and cooperation.

Then P.H. and I were dismissed.

But not before the DULL administrative assistant was instructed to make a care package for me.

P.H. and I were escorted out of DULL's central offices by Professor Hirsute-du-Vigneron. I did not want to ask about this new chair's strange behavior, though I was sorely tempted. No problem. P.H., not good at keeping things to himself, launched into an all-out explanation.

Professor Assam, it turned out, was deaf.

"Deaf?" I froze in my tracks.

"Yes," P.H. responded, "deaf."

Unlike my body, my mind was racing. So, that was the explanation for that speech I found difficult to understand. So that was the explanation for the word "extraordinary." Something in the back of my mind clicked. I had studied a foreign language (for the life of me I could not remember which one) in which the word Asamm (with a double "m" and a single "s") meant deaf. Did I dare ask P.H. about it? I had so many questions. Where would I begin? P.H. was babbling on about the incredible vision of the dean and the university administration who had had the good sense to appoint someone of Professor Assam's talents to a post like this.

The choice was actually the dean's. The administration had simply backed him up. But this had not been an easy decision, apparently.

At least not according to P.H. The dean had decided to consult with the senior faculty of Ac-Ac U. Lucky for me, this included my guide. So, there I was, privy to this inside information. The dean's motivations were very simple. A physically handicapped chairman was sure to intimidate the faculty. When confronted with him, they would consider themselves fortunate to possess their full physical faculties. I was tempted to add that this was certainly no commentary on their intellectual abilities. But I kept my mouth shut. Guilt would keep them from making too many requests. When the professors came to the chair to complain, they would be out of luck. This would spare everyone the added problems of having to deal with unruly faculty. The dean was going to have an extra benefit from this appointment, but this would only become apparent to me later.

As usual, I had too many questions. I had not learned the lesson that they try to inculcate in women. The young male who speaks at meetings or in gatherings is bright and outgoing. The young woman who does the same is obnoxious and bitchy. Women with inquiring minds must confine themselves to the *Enquirer*. For the sake of P.H., I decided to play it safe. My curiosity should be restrained. After all, as a visiting member of DULL, I would be privileged to attend departmental meetings and other functions at which I could observe Professor Assam more closely. This, I was certain, would provide me with material for a lifetime.

My briefcase loaded with DULLiana, I went home, realizing that my evening's entertainment was at hand. S. P.-T. stood at attention. Wondering what fun awaited us. She would help me read my papers, sitting on them and rubbing her body all over them.

DULL became what it is, it turns out, through some unusual forces of academic nature. A split in the university college structure had given birth to this odd child of academic specialization. A quarter of a century later, some of the founding old guard were still hanging on. Their pride and joy was giving birth to the younger generation. DULL's tenured and tenure-track population was related by more than departmental ties. Nay, let us not forget those non-tenured folks—lecturers and the like. The roster proudly displayed the names of the faculty members, followed by the name of their Ph.D.-granting institution. Surprise of surprises: why should I have been shocked? Rare was the name that was not followed by Ac-Ac U.

The situation of this department was different from anything I had seen during my ten years at Pholly U. Sure, some professors there insisted that their students be placed in their department but search committees I served on had always tried to keep academic inbreeding to a minimum.

One memo caught my eye. It addressed the No-Think Clause. I read on. The distinguishing characteristic of the male faculty members of DULL was their knowledge of languages. Thinking was out of their sphere. In fact, the administration had categorically forbidden them to think. No one knew the exact reason for this. Simply, that it had been that way all along. The old members of the department had forgotten, if they ever had known, how to think. The professors, no matter what the rank, were reminded in writing of the No-Think Clause at the beginning of every academic year. Thinking would damage the reputation of this august department within the university.

The memo was kind enough to explain that many speculations had been entertained for why this clause existed. Had someone, in the early history of the department, thought too much and gotten into trouble? Had knowledge of languages replaced other functions in the brains of these language whizzes?

The important part of this missive was highlighted. I copy it here exactly as it was in the memo:

DEAR READER. SPECULATING IS DANGEROUS. IT INVOLVES TOO MUCH THINKING. OUR ADVICE? DO NOT BECOME INVOLVED IN THIS SACRILEGIOUS ACTIVITY WHICH THREATENS THE VERY ESSENCE OF OUR DEPARTMENT. MEMORIZE OUR JINGLE. REPEAT IT TO YOURSELF ANYTIME AN ORIGINAL IDEA CROSSES YOUR MIND IN ORDER TO DISPEL IT.

> Do not think.
> Do not think.
> Help to keep us in the pink.
> New ideas are oft divisive.
> Prima donnas get derisive.
> Do not think.

I was having trouble digesting this idea. No thinking? In case I was tempted to waver, this reinforced my decision. DULL it would be.

I popped in on P.H. bright and early. I had decided to don a new pantsuit I had just bought in one of the local stores. Shopping with P.H. was not a girl's life-long dream. But what an experience! Since the faculty of Ac-Ac U. was all male but for five new women assistant professors (more on that later), the stores catering to the professional look carried, obviously, male attire. Rows and rows of suits, most of them gray or black. White shirts laid out all folded on the table. No ties were anywhere to be seen. I was intrigued and asked P.H. about this. I had been known to wear ties in my life. Not always tied like men tie them but more often thrown around my neck in a nonchalant way, giving them the look of a scarf. P.H. would not answer my inquiries, a reluctance I would come to learn about, though not fully agree with. So I bought a man's suit. After all, what is the difference between that and shopping in the men's clothing section of a department store, something I will confess to having done? (Another confession: I even owned men's shirts and men's jackets.)

In Which M/M Attends
the Open Faculty Meeting

P.H. was pleased to see me. This was the first week of classes and the university was abuzz. Telephones were ringing. Copying machines were humming. Students were in a frenzy: classes to be added, classes to be dropped. I had forgotten about the all-important first meeting of the year. P.H. handed me a copy of the flier. I remembered receiving it in my mailbox. P.H. had already warned me about the third item on the agenda. Yes. I, M/M, was the Surprise Guest.

AC-AC UNIVERSITY MEMO

TO: All Faculty, no matter what the rank
FROM: The President's Office
RE: Annual Meeting

Hark! Hark! Welcome Back to our distinguished faculty! You are invited to the first faculty meeting of the year, on Monday, xxxxxx 1, xxxx, at 3:00 p.m. We have a special agenda for you this year.

The Agenda:
1. Approval of minutes from the last meeting (Secretary of the Faculty).
2. Words of welcome (Deans).
3. Introduction of Surprise Guest (Professor Hoodwinkle).

A reception follows.

Remember: Attendance is not taken. But since all faculty members are encouraged to sit with their departments, your chairman will know whether or not you are there.

P.H. was so excited. He had, after all, taken me on as his client, despite the fact that I was a woman. The auditorium was full. The stage was lit from below and above, so that the high level administrators stepping on it looked like they were floating in a sea of light with halos on their heads.

I came in with P.H., who headed directly for the front row. Too bad. I would have preferred to be in the back, in a good position to see the multitudes of males (with the few sprinkled females) enter the room. This way at least I had a good view. We never sat down, but, like everyone else, remained standing on entering. I could sense the room filling up. Exactly on the hour, a drum roll was heard. The next thing I knew, the lights went out, we were still standing, and all eyes seemed to be riveted on the stage.

The curtains started to open and an incredible apparition was there before me. Ten young men appeared, dressed in shocking pink hot pants and with green sweaters imprinted with the logo of Ac-Ac. And what a logo it was! A turkey, face facing outward, with open arms, smiled at me. He was all in shocking pink. Set to match the color of the hot pants. Some of the young men were carrying batons, others pompoms. While I was still trying to make sense of this, P.H. whispered in my ear: "The Cheering Squad." Pink and green were the school colors.

P.H. went on to explain. This cheering squad was made up of second-year male assistant professors. They had to be nominated by their departments during their second semester at Ac-Ac U. A couple of tryouts, several practice sessions, and there were the Ac-Ac-ettes. Since, according to the school constitution, only a second-year male could be an Ac-Ac-ette, the squad changed every year.

Total silence. I am not sure whether it is the silence of awe or expectation. I do not dare inquire of P.H. the cause of this. I am silent like everyone else. All of a sudden, my ears are bombarded by a chorus of male voices resounding through the room. The tune is very familiar to me: "O Tannenbaum." I strain my ears to hear the words.

> O Great Ac-Ac.
> O Great Ac-Ac.
> We are so glad to be back.
> O Great Ac-Ac.
> O Great Ac-Ac.
> We are so glad to be back.
> Over the summer we did read.
> But colleagues' presence we do need.

O Great Ac-Ac.
O Great Ac-Ac.
We are so glad to be back.

O Great Ac-Ac.
O Great Ac-Ac.
We are so glad to be back.
O Great Ac-Ac.
O Great Ac-Ac.
We are so glad to be back.
Ahead looms another great year.
So let us cheer. So let us cheer.
O Great Ac-Ac.
O Great Ac-Ac.
We are so glad to be back.

Clapping resounded through the auditorium. The Ac-Ac-ettes disappeared and the meeting started. I had taken a pad in with me. Just in case. I had learned over the years to have paper handy during academic meetings. Male colleagues can be quite dull. Their droning voices always threatened to put me to sleep. A definite no-no. I have never met a professor who did not like the sound of his (male gender intended here) own voice. How would he then feel if he found his audience deep in the arms of Morphius? So my trusty pad was invariably there. Doodling. I was not a great artist but I liked to play with colors and shapes. And when I felt especially courageous, I would take out an assortment of pens of various colors. Red. Green. Black. Blue. Purple. Then it was doodle heaven. Not even the most boring could put me to sleep.

As soon as the clapping dies down and as soon as I can, I pull a pen from my briefcase. I am most anxious to register the words as quickly as possible, lest I lose one of them. I go over the song in my mind and I write it. How long does this take? I do not know.

Suddenly, I become aware of movement next to me. P.H. is getting up and moving to the podium. I quickly glance at the agenda in my hand. Is it possible that the two items preceding the introduction of the surprise guest have already been completed? The minutes of the last meeting are in my hands. That is no problem. I can go over them in my spare time. What about the words of welcome from the various deans? I am sorry I missed those special gems of wisdom. There will be others . . .

P.H. is now at the podium. He looks more grave than usual.

". . . a great honor . . . distinguished visitor . . . fell from the sky . . .

Ha! Ha! Ha! . . . studied with my old friend at Pholly U. . . . great books . . ."

Listening to people introduce me has always had the same effect on me. I look at them and only see their mouths moving. Their voices become disembodied entities describing this creature who it turns out is me. Often my introducers are friends. Often they are people I have just met. P.H. fit in neither group. I feel I know him well enough to judge his voice. He seems hesitant. I wonder what his dilemma might be. No matter. I also know him well enough to know that he will not be able to keep a secret and will reveal to me the reason for this.

Applause rings in my ears. This was my sign, according to P.H. who had spent long hours coaching me, to get up on the stage and say a few words. So up I went. I had spent an inordinate number of hours thinking about what I was going to say. While still a graduate student, I had been given some advice that has followed me to this fateful day at Ac-Ac U.

"Always come prepared with your paper written," my guardian angel had told me, many many moons ago.

She was right. I will admit that it is a bit anal. But it is better to be a bit—or even a lot—anal than to make an asshole of yourself.

So there I was. M/M. At Ac-Ac U. At the first faculty meeting of the year. Walking toward the stage. With my papers in my hand. I could feel all the eyes on my back. I kept walking. Up the steps. To the stage. As I turned, I looked at the audience facing me. My God. The auditorium was filled, every seat taken. Rows upon rows of male faces, some with beards, some without. Rows upon rows of male heads, some with hair, some without. But, somehow they all looked the same. Old. Young. Bald. Hairy. Their looks betrayed their curiosity.

"Thank you, Professor Hoodwinkle," I began. "It is indeed a great honor for me to be here . . ."

I continued with the nonsense I had written. I felt like a puppet reciting empty words. What I really wanted to do was laugh. Laugh at this assemblage of authority figures taking themselves so seriously. A group whose members looked the same. A group whose individuals had lost their identity. But I had decided on a tactic. I had decided to pepper my talk with meaningless words that would feed these men's egos.

"Great honor . . . eminent faculty . . . wonderful departments . . . sophisticated publications . . . great honor . . . renowned faculty . . . remarkable departments . . . ground-breaking publications . . . great honor . . . celebrated faculty . . . prominent departments . . . astounding publications . . . great honor, indeed."

More applause than I had ever been privileged to hear. And it was all for me. I must admit that I really had strained my thesaurus on this one. Would any of this honored company figure out what I had done? A question that left me a bit apprehensive.

I returned to my seat. P.H. then jumped up on the podium, full of more energy than I had seen out of him yet. My speech had obviously impressed him greatly. He thanked me. He thanked the audience. Everyone was invited to stay for a reception and meet me personally.

"Wonderful, M/M. Simply wonderful."

Multiple voices seemed to be uttering these words all at once. I did not quite know how to respond. So I stood around with a permanent smile on my face, something that seemed to make the multitude happy.

"All good things must come to an end."

P.H. really looked sad as he said this. What a cliché, I thought. But I let the poor beggar have his emotions. He clearly did not want to separate either me or himself from this distinguished company. I was still curious about his hesitation at the introductory speech. With my customary social skills, I asked him.

"Well, really, M/M. Really. I am not quite sure what you are talking about. The experience was a pleasure for me. A great pleasure, indeed. I have not introduced a woman full professor to such a distinguished company before. Quite an honor, I assure you. Quite an honor."

That did it. Now I understood. The old geezer let it out of the bag. A woman full professor, huh? So that was his problem! But he had been vindicated. There was no reason for him to be afraid. His shit-eating grin spoke quite eloquently to that. God bless my thesaurus!

In Which M/M Participates in the Induction into the Order of the Cravates

It seemed that no sooner had we finished one faculty meeting and its attendant reception than more fun was around the corner. Every fall, the president of Ac-Ac U. held a private soirée, at which recently promoted faculty were inducted into the Order of the Cravates. Only senior faculty were invited. What luck! P.H. had also gotten me an engraved invitation. I held on to it as one would a very precious object, reading it over and over again. This was obviously such a sacred occasion that not even the Ac-Ac-ettes were permitted to attend. For this one, I really could not restrain my curiosity. P.H. be damned. To my surprise, he delighted in my desire to know about this obviously important event. As for the Ac-Ac-ettes,

"Too junior, you know. Simply too junior. And certainly not sophisticated enough."

This milestone I understood to be the crowning glory of Ac-Ac U. It had to be held early in the academic year, preferably before the first faculty meeting so that the recent promotees could enjoy their new rank and parade themselves appropriately. But since the president, who must officiate at this function, was held up on a trip, the first faculty meeting had taken place before the Induction. The poor beggars had to wait a few extra days for their goodies. Life is cruel, indeed.

Here, P.H. was careful to tell me, I would finally understand the system of hierarchies so dear to Ac-Ac U. The invitation was actually quite cryptic. It was merely gracious words from the high muck-muck of Ac-Ac U. inviting me to this closed ceremony. Period.

Let us face it. This was not an event. This was a rite of passage. So I donned my new dress outfit. A black velvety pantsuit with a white silk shirt. I had bought a black and white scarf, what someone back at the old Pholly U. would surely call a power scarf. And off I went with P.H. to the president's house. This poor man had had his ears filled with me. He had already had to clear the Guest House for S. P.-T. And now this. Well, he does get paid handsomely. So there.

P.H. and I stepped into a most elegant room. Our invitations had been checked at the door. 8:00 p.m. was the beginning of this honored event. It was only 7:55. Everyone was standing at attention. In total silence. Chairs, facing a dais, lined the room. But not simple chairs. They were of two types: leather and cloth. The front two rows had three black leather easy chairs each, and the next two rows had six brown leather easy chairs each. The remainder of the room was filled with easy chairs, but these were covered with cloth. We, like those already present, stood in front of the cloth-covered chairs. No one could sit until the president of Ac-Ac U., Professor Arnoldo Salvatore Schmeergang, had entered the room.

I had by now heard so much about Schmeergang's humble beginnings that I could have probably recited the entire saga on my own. His father had insisted on naming him Arnoldo with an "o" and not an "a" to break the family tradition. To give his son a chance to be different from all the other Arnaldos in the family. And becoming a college president was certainly different. The spelling of his name was now a matter of pride for Ac-Ac U.'s president.

I had not yet met him but this had to wait until the completion of the ceremony. His entrance was to be grand and his first words would be addressed to the promotees. In fact, he is the only one permitted to speak during this formal occasion. The room was beginning to fill up. P.H., in his usual way, was whispering needed information to me. The promotees were in two separate rooms off the living room. They would be ushered in one group at a time. The promoters, however, were all there, standing at attention along with everyone else. Needless to say, I was the only woman in the room.

8:00 p.m. All the male heads surrounding me seem to turn in one motion toward a door to my right. The door slowly opens and in walks a middle-aged (I have always been bad at guessing ages) man. Dressed in, what else, a black suit, a white shirt, and, of all things, a black bow tie. He stands by himself on the dais, facing the crowd. The dais has no chair. Simply the erect body of the Ac-Ac U. President, Arnoldo Salvatore Schmeergang.

"Welcome one. Welcome all."

His voice resounds throughout the room. I wonder how often he has done this.

"We will begin with the GTs."

The GTs? What are the GTs? I had not heard anything about that before. My mind was trying to take in all the sights while at the same time tackling this new concept. No matter. I would find out quickly enough.

No sooner had President Schmeergang finished his words than an older professor (I had met him but could not remember his name) opened a door and ushered in six white-haired but nevertheless balding gentlemen, wearing black suits and white shirts. No ties? I was very confused. This is very much unlike the code at Ac-Ac U. P.H. was no longer whispering to me. The occasion had become much too solemn. Little does he know that I have promised myself to accost him afterward.

The six are seated in the six black leather chairs, their bodies seeming to merge with the chairs themselves. As soon as they are seated, we all sit.

"This is a most solemn time for Ac-Ac U.," President Schmeergang begins. "We are here to induct six new professors into our highest rank, the rank of the Groin Ties."

Had I misunderstood Schmeergang? Did he say Groin Ties? Was he talking about the sounds pigs make? I was completely confused.

He was continuing.

"They have achieved this through a rigorous process of secret evaluation. I speak on behalf of the entire university community when I say that this is a great honor for all those involved, including myself. How well do I remember my own Induction into the Order of the Cravates. For you, the new GTs, wear this rank well. You are the pride and joy of this glorious institution."

President Schmeergang then stepped down from the dais and started to walk toward the rows of seated bald heads. The professor who had ushered the fortunate six new GTs reappeared carrying in his arms six enormously long black boxes. Almost simultaneously with these events, and with one motion, the six new inductees stood. The boxes also started their own movement. The guide would hand one carefully to the president who would then place it just as carefully into the extended arms of the awaiting GT. Six times.

Then President Schmeergang returned to the dais.

"Open!," his voice resounded once more.

Six black boxes were suddenly uncovered and their contents revealed. Long black ties!

"Wear these well," Schmeergang advised. "It is my duty and pleasure to help each and everyone of you, should it prove necessary, in tying his Groin Tie so that it will be the right length. I will personally see to it that the exact position of the Groin Tie is where it should be. After all, each of you now is a Professor-ès-Groin and only the length of the tie will make this clear."

The usher-cum-tie-deliverer came in rolling a full-length mirror, which was placed next to the dais. One by one, the new GTs were escorted to the mirror and to the loving proximity of Schmeergang. It was time to tie these infamous Groin Ties. One by one, these distinguished professors (truly, this word now befitted them, for they had reached Ac-Ac U.'s highest rank) proceeded to the tying process. The tie was fortunately long enough. But the point was to have it reach the groin.

So that's what the title meant! Five of the six promotees extricated themselves quite well, succeeding in this task on the first round. The sixth one was not so adept. He was wearing exceptionally thick eyeglasses, and this may have hindered his progress. No matter. Schmeergang came to the rescue. I could tell he was concerned lest this new promotee leave the ceremony uncertain about the placement of the Groin Tie.

Now there were these six new Professors-ès-Groin (I was not sure whether to pluralize the Groins here or not—at least it will give the specialists in the French language something to worry about). Ties tied, clearly full of themselves, the six returned to their chairs as President Schmeergang headed back to the dais.

"We will end with the BTs," boomed Schmeergang's voice.

I decided not to wonder what the BTs were. I was sure Schmeergang would utter the magic words somewhere along the line.

There was the usher-cum-tie-deliverer once more opening the magic door. This time, he ushered in twelve somberly dressed younger professors. That is, they were younger in relative terms. Most looked like they were close to fifty. They were dressed in dark brown suits and white shirts. Again, no ties. I did not wonder about that on this round.

"Welcome, dear colleagues, in our midst," Arnoldo Salvatore Schmeergang began.

I had to keep myself from yawning. Could I stay awake through yet another set of platitudes? I wondered what S. P.-T. was up to. She did not like to be left alone in our limited space in the Guest House. When I came home after these deadly occasions, she would rub her head all over my legs and ask me where I had been.

"Sorry, little one. You know I have to do this."

This was our normal routine. S. P.-T. really put up with a lot from me.

". . . twelve new professors into the great rank of the Belly Button Ties."

The words Belly Button brought me back to Ac-Ac U. Thank God that Schmeergang had decided to put such emphasis on these two words. Had he not, I might have dozed off, and think of how embarrassing that would have been. Not just for myself but for poor P.H. I had, nevertheless, missed the opening of Schmeergang's speech. Life is full of lost opportunities . . .

At least, this time, I did not wonder about the words Belly Button and whether or not I had misunderstood our fearless leader. After all, if Groins were the top of the planet here, was it not natural for Belly Buttons to be next in line?

He was continuing.

"They have achieved this through a rigorous process of secret evaluation. I speak on behalf of the entire university community when I say that this is a great honor for all those involved, including myself. How well do I remember my own Induction into the Order of the Cravates. For you, the new BTs, wear this rank well. You are the pride and joy of this glorious institution."

Interesting. It sounded so familiar. But I had not written the earlier perorations down and so I could not tell if he had merely repeated himself. But if he had, all the better. It would mean that I had not missed much of his verbiage on my earlier mental wanderings. I had not brought along a pad for this solemn evening. Doodling would have been a no-no.

As before, President Schmeergang proceeded from the dais toward the new promotees. Once again, the professor acting as master of ceremonies appeared, but this time carrying twelve not so enormously long black boxes. The twelve new inductees stood up.

If the words are the same, why should not the actions be? Repetition was as important as the rite itself. It doubly instilled values. There was Schmeergang handing out boxes with ties once more. There was the mirror rolled in once more. And there was the tying ceremony. Was it age? Was it excitement? All twelve new promotees handled their ties beautifully. Schmeergang's instructions be damned. Somehow, they all seemed to have just the right instinct about the placement of the tie. Nevertheless, Schmeergang's voice boomed out. His words were adamant.

"Being a Belly Button Professor represents a high degree of responsibility. It is possibly the most difficult of the promotions at Ac-Ac U. I beseech all of you to remember precisely where your Belly Button Tie should lie. The end of the tie should reach that exalted part of the body. Make it a bit short or make it a bit long and you have lost the game. For then you risk intruding on the next rank. Remember, I am always ready and prepared to take time out from my busy schedule to help you with this problem, should you need it. Welcome, my dear colleagues and friends, to your new esteemed rank at Ac-Ac U."

This seemed to signal the end of the ceremony for those in the know. Shoulders relaxed. Bodies began to converge toward the new promotees. Even President Schmeergang was showing signs of having completed an important and grave task. He was patting the lucky candidates on the back. A sort of more informal welcome to the club.

I stood and looked around. Faces were beaming. Those of the promotees and others. I think I understood what each new inductee was feeling. At least concerning the promotion. P.H. had explained to me quite eloquently and at length that once you were in the Order of the Cravates, your academic future at Ac-Ac U. was assured. It was understandable. After all, being a Belly Button Tie meant that you were secure in the knowledge that your life was taken care of. Whether you became a Groin Tie was ultimately up to you. To work or not to work. That was the question. People retired at Ac-Ac U. as Belly Buttoners. I could not help but think that that was a sign of hope.

Who should then start toward me but his eminence himself, President Arnoldo Salvatore Schmeergang. I sensed this would involve yet more words of welcome so I braced myself and plastered my face with an enormous smile. I was a product of Pholly U. after all, was I not? I had been trained, if you please, in high academic politics.

"Ah. M/M. That is M slash M, is it not?"

"Yes," I heard myself saying.

Quick, M/M, show your stuff.

"How nice it is to finally meet you, President Schmeergang."

"Likewise. Likewise, my dear."

His dear? What makes him think I am his dear? I know. I know. These are meaningless phrases. But, please. I could not in a million years call him "my dear." So, what's in a name, you say? Plenty. I let him go on, however.

"Welcome to Ac-Ac U. I extend the heartiest of welcomes to you. I am sure I speak on behalf of all my wonderful and distinguished colleagues when I say that it is a great honor to have you in our midst."

Fortunately, P.H. had warned me that I should not so much as dream of interrupting Schmeergang once he got started. So I stood at attention. The honored president would signal me when he finished his words of wisdom by patting me on the back. At least that was his habit with male colleagues. P.H. was not sure how the gender issue would play there. He was most interested, as I was, in seeing what President Arnoldo Salvatore Schmeergang would do. Would he pat the distinguished female visitor on her back? If so, would this action be an expression of his philosophy on women at Ac-Ac U.? Or would he refrain from doing something that might compromise his feelings in any way? I could sense the tension in the room. I was surprised that no one had taken bets. Had the enormity of the occasion struck Schmeergang?

"This is indeed a wonderful opportunity for our fine university to have someone of your stature with us. Professor Hoodwinkle has spoken to me of you with great admiration."

I was about to respond that P.H. was certainly a sly one was he not? But I caught myself in time.

"I understand from Professor Hoodwinkle that you have great administrative experience. That you have served on many important committees at Pholly U."

Would that I could respond to Schmeergang's comments! Would that I could share my committee experiences with him! But is he really interested in them?

"As you may know, I am trying to move this institution forward. As you may also know, Ac-Ac U. is in its infancy as regards women academics. This is an issue that is very dear to my heart. There are, however, many problems we need to overcome before we ask them to join us in our distinguished institution. I, like many of the senior faculty here, am concerned that should women join our ranks, they will be unhappy. Everything has its own time. Everything has to be made perfect for their integration in the Ac-Ac academy. Ha! Ha!"

Obviously, this was some kind of a word play President Schmeergang was indulging in. Should I join him in his own good humor? I was uncertain about the hierarchical etiquette for this kind of occasion. I decided to take my cue from the assembled company. No one had participated with the august president in his own merriment. So there I was once again sealing my lips. This was turning into a disturbing habit.

"I am hoping that your presence will be an inspiration for us, M/M. That you will help us with your great wisdom and administrative skills. I have long been an admirer of Pholly U. and of the administration's courage in implementing certain measures not popular among the faculty."

I was not sure what he meant but I was slowly going crazy listening to him. His general philosophy was distasteful to me. His arguments were familiar and outdated. The "you need to have perfect circumstances before anything can be done" argument. I had fought against it my entire life.

I was hesitating. Watching. Listening. Finally, I decided to take the bull by the horns. I had nothing to lose. I spoke.

"Precisely what do you mean, President Schmeergang?"

Have I seen P.H. ever look so shocked? I don't think so. Had I learned that he and all his distinguished colleagues had shat in their pants right on the spot, I would not have been surprised. No one in the history of President Schmeergang's presidency had ever interrupted him before his friendly pat on the back. No one. And a woman to boot?

President Arnoldo Salvatore Schmeergang did not look too happy himself. What could he do? Not give me tenure? Kick me off the hallowed academic grounds of Ac-Ac U.? We cannot all afford to be academic wet noodles.

"Well. Hm . . . Hm . . . You have taken me completely by surprise, M/M."

And it is about time, I was tempted to say.

"I suppose it is only fair. After all, I am the one who likes to shake things up. I think I am going to like you, M/M. You see, my dear..." *(Oh, no. Not him too, again. For how many of them was I going to be the dear over and over?)* "What I meant was simply that I have long been an admirer of Pholly U. In fact, if its administration were to offer me the presidency of that great institution, they would be bestowing a great honor on me. Mind you, I do not normally reveal this sort of information to everyone. But, here, the assembled company is the best that Ac-Ac U. has to offer. So I am sure they do not mind my sharing it with you."

I was trying to fathom what President Schmeergang was trying to say to me. What does the distinction of Pholly U. have to do with the argument concerning women at Ac-Ac U.? Was he cruising for a position at my own Pholly U.? This time, I told myself, I had better not repeat the stunt of interrupting this highest of all possible administrators at Ac-Ac U.

"Given the great distinction of your home institution, and given your own distinction," *(God, this word was getting on my nerves)* "you can well understand our desire to have you advise us on these matters. I would, therefore, be very grateful if you would agree to serve on some very prestigious and important committees while you are at Ac-Ac U."

This was not a question. It was a request one did not refuse. Imagine my surprise when President Arnoldo Salvatore Schmeergang then lifted his right arm and directed it to my back. Slap—or more appropriately—pat. Was this the much-awaited signal? I assumed it was.

Great commotion followed Schmeergang's action. I was surrounded. P.H.'s mouth was twitching. In fact, if I was not mistaken, his entire body was shaking. Certainly, I had never seen him like this. I could understand it. I, his protégé, had wreaked havoc in his existence by breaking the most important code at Ac-Ac U.: silence in front of authority. Would he be able to live down the embarrassment of my act? Schmeergang, on the other hand, was taking the whole thing in stride. I think that he actually enjoyed it.

"Well, M/M, what do you say?" This was President Schmeergang.

"Well, Sir, I don't quite know what to say."

How is that for a response? An answer that was patterned on the noble president's question. There was enough modesty in it to guarantee that I would not be a threat. That "Sir" was to make him feel powerful.

"It is, of course, a great honor that you are bestowing on me and on Pholly University."

The addition of the institution always got to them.

"I will be more than pleased to help out in any way I can. Your generosity and hospitality have been wonderful. Just let me know what you would like me to do."

P.H. was beginning to look a bit more relaxed. The dire consequences of my act were clearly not so dire. Everyone was milling around. He himself was being accosted by colleagues. In the flurry of my unnatural act, the professorial company had almost forgotten about the promotees. They were standing around, trying to look normal. A difficult thing to do when one is supposed to be the center of attention and somehow is not. So I started moving toward them. Congratulating them. Assuring them that this was a great occasion, indeed, and a great honor for me. To be permitted to share in their memorable moment.

The new Professors-ès-Groin were having the greatest difficulty assimilating all this. Or so at least it seemed to me from the stares and glares they were directing at me. After all, they had just acceded to the highest rank their institution could bestow on them. This was their moment in the sun. And it had been kidnapped by no less than this woman visitor, who dropped down from the sky to disturb their universe. To add insult to injury, she had just broken one of the cardinal rules of the institution. And what are these rules for if not to guarantee the hierarchy that they had all been trained for so long to respect and even to love? I could almost hear them saying to themselves: If President Schmeergang can be interrupted by this intruder, what will happen to us? I wanted to scream at them. To shake them from their lethargy and to guarantee them that they had nothing to fear from me.

But, I suppose, once a castrating female, always a castrating female.

This would be a great moment for me to exit this distinguished company, I decided. Leave the boys alone to plot for a bit, should they choose to. Claiming exhaustion from this emotionally draining and exciting evening, I begged President Schmeergang's indulgence and proceeded toward the door. I wanted at all cost to avoid P.H. No "You should not have done that" tonight. I did not feel I could cope with it. But, P.H. was too fast for me. I saw his shape advancing toward me.

"A great occasion, M/M. A great occasion. Must you leave? We will talk about all this some more."

"A great occasion, indeed."

I had discovered over the years that people love to hear their own words repeated to them. A validation of sorts. P.H. was no exception.

"And thank you again, Professor Hoodwinkle, for allowing me to share in it."

I took this exchange to mean that P.H. was not too dissatisfied. Could that glint in his eyes even be betraying some hidden pleasure at what had transpired? His promises to talk about things fortunately never materialized. I had become accustomed to that.

In Which M/M Feels Over-Received

Aside from being such an obviously distinguished institution, Ac-Ac U. had the honor of being the university with the greatest number of beginning-of-year receptions it had been my very mitigated pleasure to attend. The new college faculty were received by the dean. The new university faculty were received by the president and the deans. The new faculty and librarians along with their families were received by the various university dignitaries. It all took my breath away. Seas of smiling faces littered with white name tags bearing the school seal: pink turkey rampant on a field of green.

I stood and stood. The faces were beginning to have that familiarity that one becomes accustomed to in other public places. Gyms. That is what it made me think of. But this was mental exercise instead of physical exercise. One circulated much as one does in the gyms. Waiting to talk to the president. Like waiting for a machine to open up. Then one had one's turn and it was on to someone else. I kept my smile plastered and decided to watch rather than participate. Infinitely more interesting.

Schmeergang was an old pro at this. I even caught him winking at me as he hustled his way across the nervous huddles of new faculty. How young they all looked! How desperate they were to impress the university officials! Was I like this I wondered? Had I looked so nervous when I started my career? I somehow doubted it. I was not a shy one. At least, not by the time I had climbed over all the hurdles and received my multiple bruises.

My least favorite reception? The one at Schmeergang's house. Without a doubt. He gets the gold star on that one. I shook so many hands that I was sure my arm would fall off. And then there were the old geezers who truly had never set eyes on a female academic before. And one wearing pants to boot. To say that they gave me dirty looks would be an understatement. Some of them even tripped and bumped into one another as they walked past me, eyes fixated on me instead of on the direction they were going.

P.H. was there. Of course.

"Isn't this grand, M/M? I must confess to you that it warms my heart to see all these eager new faces. Fine additions to Ac-Ac U. Every one of them."

Sure. Sure. I was tempted to reply.

Perhaps for the first time in my entire academic career, I actually felt a bit of nostalgia for Pholly U. Frankly, it made me a bit sick to my stomach. But when I realized that it was only because good old Pholly U. distinguished itself by the absence of receptions, I felt better.

P.H.'s words were my cue.

"This has been most interesting, Professor Hoodwinkle. But my companion awaits me. So I shall say good-bye."

In Which M/M Decides Which Course to Audit

Wow. I, unlike P.H., am quite glad that these good things come to an end. And so it was that I finally arrived at the Guest House. I felt like a caged animal whose prison bars had finally been opened. I uttered a long sigh of relief as I entered my room. And there was S. P.-T. to greet me, purring and rubbing against my legs.

"Well, our work is cut out for us, little one. We must choose what courses to audit. But, first, some well-deserved rest."

I needed to clear my head of the Induction Ceremony before choosing a course to audit. This is where that load of DULL papers would finally come in handy. I could not decide whether to start with the faculty list and the description of their specialties or with the course descriptions. S. P.-T. was keenly chewing on the course booklet, a garish red affair. So that decided it for me.

There we were, S. P.-T. and I, some hours later, absorbed in the course booklet. The wealth of DULL courses was beyond compare. Where do I start? Pages and pages of promised knowledge. Secrets of the DULL universe. Much to my surprise (and pleasure I should add) I found that DULL was quite an imperialist little department. Any course that could have some relevance found its way to the DULL course booklet and was decorated with a DULL course number.

The list of the courses was in the front of the booklet. I was actually disappointed that there were only three courses that struck my fancy: "The Art of Reciting the Dictionary," "Reading between the Lines," and "Sleeping through the Ages." Each represented a different wing of the department. Each guaranteed results and promised to unlock doors of knowledge to the unsuspecting student.

1. "The Art of Reciting the Dictionary"
   Staff
   Course Purpose: To train the student to memorize and recite entries from the dictionary of his choice. Shorter dictionaries are encouraged.

Since DULL covered many languages, this course rotated among the faculty. I could not conceive of sitting in a classroom trying to learn how to memorize a dictionary. This course might justify DULL's acronym. S. P.-T. had walked away from the booklet. I took this as a sign.

So it was on to the next course.

2.   "Reading between the Lines: On Reading a Text: Letters, Words, and Numbers."
     Professor Seymour Flabgrass

Professor Flabgrass had been wise enough not to provide a course description. I remembered some tidbits from P.H.'s description of DULL. At the time I had not paid much attention. Now it was beginning to come back. Professor Flabgrass had always taken the English language seriously. He firmly believed that metaphorical interpretations ruined "our fine native tongue," as he fondly called it, and denuded it of its purity. His unorthodox views had earned him a certain amount of fame among the more well-known Ac-Ac U. faculty.

Reading between the lines meant for him literally to read between the lines. Spaces turned into significant entities. The spatial ups and downs created by the conjunction of one letter being on top of the other added to the mystery. One could carry the analysis into hitherto unknown areas: the length of words, the spacing. Obviously, his theory could be applied to any language. All one needed was some rudiments of the Flabgrassian theory of reading between the lines and off one could go. This explained the presence of the course in the DULL booklet.

A side benefit of the Flabgrassian theory was that its inventor had somehow attached it to a complicated numerical system in which letters and words were calculated. One had to count the number of consonants and vowels in a word. Even-numbered words were auspicious, uneven ones were bad luck. In dire cases, the Flabgrassian theory provided for great flexibility: certain letters, like the "m" or "w" could count as one letter or as two, depending on the need. In exceptional cases, apostrophes and hyphens could count as well. What a theory! Seymour Flabgrass had apparently justly earned his fame among his Ac-Ac U. colleagues.

I had already decided when P.H. was explaining all this to me that this would most likely not be a subject of great fascination to me. Seeing the title cured any remnant of a desire I might have had lurking in the back of my mind to audit the Flabgrassian course. I was really allergic to double colons.

Language. Literature. My head was spinning with the DULL list of courses. I wondered how the students fared when confronted with all this material.

"We are down to one last option, S. P.-T."

At this point, my trusty friend, perhaps much smarter than I, had long given up on the DULL course booklet and was sitting watching me bemusedly as if to tell me that I was insane to indulge in this activity. Since there was only that third possibility left, I decided to go on. Where would my mad adventures to find a course to audit lead me?

3. "Sleeping through the Ages"
   Professor Hergé Somnanbule
   Sleep is by far the most important activity. Otherwise, why would we all spend approximately a third of our lives sleeping? The purpose of this course is to investigate the intimate relationship that exists between the activity of sleeping and major historical events or moments. "Ages" is being understood not only in its historical meaning but in its other significations, including the biological one.

Thus did Professor Somnanbule begin his course description. This was certainly a promising beginning. S. P.-T. must have known in advance what this course was about. There she was, face to the ground, eyes closed, sleeping.

Did Napoleon have a good night's sleep before the battle of Austerlitz? Did Attila the Hun snore? Do older and younger people sleep the same number of hours? These and other questions will occupy our attention for part of this course. Students will be exposed to literary texts, to cinematic production, to art that all in one way or another deal with sleeping and with its historical and cultural influence.

So far, so good. I was having a hard time imagining where Professor Somnanbule would go next with his course description.

The other side of this course is the practical one. The professor will demonstrate different positions for sleeping. The students will then themselves be given an opportunity to test these positions by sleeping through a segment of the class.

The appeal of this course is obvious. Each of us is under the obligation of knowing more about a most important human activity.

No one would dream (excuse the pun) of arguing with Professor Somnanbule's logic here. I debated with myself. This might be a course worth auditing. The question was whether after ten years at Pholly U. I really could sit and listen to someone like Somnanbule, whose very name put me to sleep.

P.H. had already told me that Somnanbule was one of the most popular professors at Ac-Ac U. and had won the most prestigious teaching award the university offered. Now I understood the reason for his popularity. What undergraduate in his (or even her) right mind would not want to take a course in which much of the class time involved sleeping? I read further and discovered that Somnanbule had scheduled the class at 8:00 in the morning. Ghastly. I simply do not function that early. That would have to decide it. If the time had not made me hesitate, the location would have. "Sleeping through the Ages" was held in one of the biggest auditoriums on campus.

The more I thought about it, the more unpleasant the idea of sitting in on this course became. I hate crowds. Why else would I have gone off in the hot air balloon all alone? I would undoubtedly have to arrive at the auditorium early to assure myself a seat. P.H. had indicated that this course had a waiting list. It vied in popularity and in numbers with a course on "Meditation" in the Department of Ecstasy.

This was in a sense a false problem for me. P.H. had reassured me when the idea of my auditing a course came up that he would personally speak to the professor in charge of whatever course appealed to me and guarantee me a place. With "Sleeping through the Ages," this would pose problems of its own. Did I really want to show up and always sit in the same reserved seat? If the reserved seat were in the front of the auditorium, as it would most likely be, how could I effectively watch the students? The hell with Hergé Somnanbule. I might ask him for the syllabus and his packet of readings if the fancy strikes me later on. For now, however, he would have to sit beside the other rejects.

I had trouble believing that I had actually been unable to find a single course that would hold my interest. Were my standards too rigorous? I was beginning to wonder. I decided to give the course booklet another go. And so down the list I went. No. No surprises. This decision might have to be revised, but for now I would occupy myself with various other activities.

In Which M/M Goes through the Faculty List at DULL in Search of Someone

Confess it, M/M. I do confess. I do confess. I have always *loved* reading biographies. It did not matter really who the people were. Intellectual gossip of sorts. I imagined what the individuals looked like. I imagined what their lives were like. I imagined all sorts of things about them that may have had nothing to do with their reality.

True, the course list had been rather unproductive. But faculty lists were another matter. The DULL list on first glance did not look true to the department's acronym: it provided mini-biographies of the various intellectual leaders of that august department. So down the alphabet I went. Skipping gaily through the totally unexciting biographies. Forget Somnanbule's course. The DULL faculty list was a most efficacious soporific.

The Someone I was looking for did not exist. There was not a truly outstanding faculty member on the list. Maybe the list is outdated, I told myself. I decided to go back to the DULL administrative offices first thing in the morning and speak to Assam's administrative assistant. Why not take her to lunch? She undoubtedly knows more about the department than any of its faculty members.

In Which M/M Has a Heart to Heart Talk with Herself about Her Future at Ac-Ac U.

There I am. Sitting in the Ac-Ac U. Guest House. S. P.-T. is looking at me, wondering what I am planning. I am not sure. When P.H. had initially proposed this visiting position, it seemed the perfect break from an otherwise dull routine at Pholly U. Now here I am. My ideas are not generating much interest, not even in me. There are no courses to audit. True, there would be committees. There were still departmental meetings to regale me. True, I could interview individual faculty. I had not yet met the dean. And there are things that still intrigue me about Ac-Ac U. Take it one day at a time, I told myself. I was quite upset about the women faculty and wondered if Schmeergang meant what he said. So Ac-Ac U. would have another chance. Lunch it would be with DULL's administrative assistant.

In Which M/M Meets the Dean

"Forgive me, M/M."

What was the old twit talking about?

P.H. was clearly flustered. We had arranged our usual meeting and there he was in quite a state.

"I have neglected my duties. I should have set up your interview with the dean earlier. How can you function without that?"

I was about to respond: "Quite well, thank you." But remember, I told myself, a learning mission is a learning mission!

"You are right, Professor Hoodwinkle. So when do I meet this legendary personality?"

"Tsk. Tsk. You must allow me to impart some of my wisdom to you, M/M. To talk of the dean in this way is highly improper. Dean Hendrick Gloopersnort is a unique dean. He is an unqualified supporter of your department."

"My department?"

"DULL, my dear."

My department? Did I become a member of this distinguished group so quickly? I found the idea frightening.

"You will see, M/M, that without his helping hand, DULL would never have existed. Enough of that for now. Dean Gloopersnort personally telephoned me requesting this meeting. He is a great fan of your oratory."

I must have looked confused.

"He was there when you delivered those fine words at the first faculty meeting."

Oh, yes. I had almost forgotten. My thesaurus twister!

"We have a meeting with Dean Gloopersnort immediately."

Off we went. Gaily plodding our way through layers and layers of students lying about on the grass and the walkways throughout the campus. A nice day at Ac-Ac U. always brought them out.

The building in which Dean Hendrick Gloopersnort's office was housed was in a central location on the Ac-Ac U. campus. Up an elevator. And there a double door led into the sacred enclosure: Gloopersnort's hide-out. A young office assistant, whom I would discover later was a student working his way through school, motioned us to sit down.

Dean Gloopersnort, it seemed, was delayed by an urgent long distance phone call. Good. This would give me the chance to drink in the surroundings. Plush leather chairs. Walls overflowing with painted portraits of previous holders of Gloopersnort's office. Appropriately dressed in the regimental dark suit with white shirt and tie. All smiling beatifically. As if they had just had an orgasm. As if they had finally reached a state of ultimate satisfaction.

Gloopersnort was rich in staff. Younger secretaries. Older secretaries. Working students. All were obviously at his beck and call. No sooner would a telephone ring than it would be picked up. Forms were exchanging hands.

Our arrival had already been announced. P.H. and I sat facing Gloopersnort's door. Anxiously awaiting its opening. The door perhaps read our minds. It seemed to open of its own free will before we noticed the form of Dean Hendrick Gloopersnort appearing through it. A short man dressed like his predecessors. Those powerful ancestors whose eyes were constantly on him. Why should I have been surprised?

"Welcome, young lady." (*Shit. Not again.*) "Welcome. And by all means, please honor my office with your presence."

Slick character. But will these assholes ever stop it? I really thought that I would scream this time. P.H. must have seen the look of fury in my eyes because he made a very subtle hand movement, trying to calm me down. The episode with Schmeergang had taught me a lesson. Do not sit or stand by, as the case may be.

"My name is M/M."

"Oh. Yes. I know. Welcome, M/M." A charming smile appeared on his semi-wrinkled face. He was blushing a bit. I finally caught one of these bastards with his pants down.

He put out his hand to shake mine. At the same time, there emanated from his mouth, in a slow, dreamy-like voice, the words:

"Let us go . . ."

My hand was still in his. I wondered what the hell was going on. Was this a pass? I did not know what to say. Another explosion from his mouth penetrated my ears, saving me.

"Then, you and I,"

It was like a bolt of lightening. I could not suppress a smile. How can I have forgotten P.H.'s words?

"Our dean is an extraordinarily learned and talented young man. True, he is a scientist. Chemistry, to be precise. But he is extremely knowledgeable in the humanities. In fact, given that about half of his publications are related to humanistic topics, such as language and literature, we consider him one of ours."

So, come on, M/M, fast on your feet. I heard my own voice reciting back to this creature still holding my hand:

"When the evening is spread out against the sky."

My hand was released. A boom of laughter greeted me and this all-powerful figure that is Gloopersnort, wearing a GT, motioned me to a chair. P.H. was an outside observer of this rather unexpected exchange. I sat down. Dean Gloopersnort moved himself behind his desk and very nonchalantly placed his feet on the desk. Was this a challenge? The ease with which he did it probably meant that the act was part of his normal routine.

This seemingly young dean (actually I discovered later that he was not as young as he looked—his hair was clearly dyed, he had obviously had a face lift) was a big fan of T. S. Eliot. Lucky was the candidate who successfully passed this heroic test, this important rite of passage that signaled great future fortune. Obviously, I had passed the test. What would have happened, I wondered, if I had been unable to respond with the right line? Would my hand still be in Dean Gloopersnort's hand? What a frightening thought!

"This is a wonderful opportunity for the College, M/M, to have you join—if only on a temporary basis—our distinguished Department of Unusual Languages and Literatures."

I had heard this so often that my vomit reflex was by now desensitized.

"Your words at the Faculty meeting impressed me greatly . . ."

I thought to myself that despite his position, this was yet another brainless wonder.

"I realize that you could have chosen many another department in many another college. We, indeed, are the fortunate ones who will benefit from your presence amongst us. It will be my privilege to have you as my guest at chairmen's meetings and at various receptions sponsored by the college. I will personally make sure that my staff sends you the proper engraved invitations. And, of course, since Professor Hoodwinkle is an eminent participant at these functions, I trust that he will assure your presence there. I understand from President Arnoldo Schmeergang that you have kindly agreed to sit on some of our more important committees. I, like President Schmeergang, will be extremely grateful for your insights. If there is anything I can do for you while you are in our midst, please do not hesitate to let me know. My office will be permanently at your disposal."

Dean Hendrick Gloopersnort's legs started to move off the table even before he had finished his last sentence. This was the signal for P.H. and me. We were being dismissed from the premises of the deanery.

After the empty niceties, P.H. and I eased our way out of Dean Gloopersnort's suite of offices.

"Professor Hoodwinkle," I began, "these meetings with top-level administrators are flattering. But I am most anxious to meet the women faculty."

"Of course, M/M. Of course. I will arrange a meeting as quickly as possible."

In Which M/M Takes Steps to Set Up the Legendary Meeting with the Women Faculty at Ac-Ac U.

"As quickly as possible." These were P.H.'s actual words. But moving slowly was his specialty. I had forgotten how ineffective someone can be when that someone does not wish to do a job. P.H. clearly did not want me to meet the women faculty. Over and over, on a daily basis, I had to remind him of his promise. The excuses varied. It was difficult to schedule a time at which everyone could meet. It was difficult to find an appropriate location. After all, only the best would do for M/M. The best be damned, I finally had to tell him. I simply wanted to meet the women faculty. What was wrong with that?

Back and forth. Back and forth. This may have been one of the most difficult tasks I had ever set myself. The problem seemed insurmountable. I could not help but think that some malice was involved here. The bastards had never been able to stop me before. Why should they do so now?

Sitting home one night with S. P.-T. and talking it over with her, the solution came to me. Like a flash. Why not have the women faculty over to my suite at the Guest House for an evening of wine and cheese? I am not a big socializer myself. In fact, I have already confessed to having been accused of misanthropy. There was probably some truth to that. S. P.-T., on the other hand, loved company. And company loved her. She was beautiful. That helped. Calico colors of various shades of brown with generous sprinklings of white. Her eyes had more intelligence than the eyes of many of my colleagues. A particularly astute friend of mine declared to me one day that she felt S. P.-T. could speak to her. Why not, in fact?

I presented the solution to P.H. To say that he was flabbergasted would be an understatement. His entire body was unable to express the variety and depth of emotions he felt. His arms and hands twitched. He looked as if he were going to lose his balance. And this is not to speak of his face! It was as if I had just informed him that a woman had landed at Ac-Ac U. from outer space. Actually worse. After all, that had happened with my arrival, had it not, and he and his cohorts had survived it. There was fear here, deep deep fear. Of what I do not understand. After all, what did he expect me to do to these women?

"Eh . . . Eh . . . That does seem to be an interesting idea, M/M."

I could tell that P.H. was choosing his words carefully. "Interesting" is one of the most wonderfully innocuous adjectives ever adopted by academics. One could use it as a stop gap. For lack of anything else to say. For not wanting to express one's opinion. P.H. was leaving his options open.

"But really, M/M, I am not sure about the logistics. How do we work it out? Will the women faculty be able to attend without a problem? If we hold this gathering at night, will those who have classes the next day be able to attend? Oh, dear. Oh, dear. You have certainly come up with an interesting idea, M/M. Yes, an interesting idea, indeed."

This was going to be more difficult than I had anticipated. P.H.'s resistance was greater than I had assumed it would be. He was fairly representative of the male administrative powers at Ac-Ac U.

"Really, now, Professor Hoodwinkle."

I had to respond quickly. I did not want to give him too much time to come up with more excuses.

"I think these problems could be easily solved. After all, we are only talking about five women faculty members here. Why not give me their names and phone numbers and I will try to arrange the meeting myself?"

Another thunderbolt. If I threw any more at P.H., he would surely kill me. Poor man. I did feel sorry for him. Was it his fault that he happened to be on the beach at the moment my hot air balloon crashed? Was it his fault that he had a sudden generous urge to host this creature from outer space? Well, maybe it is. Maybe he is simply paying for the sins of his gender.

"Another interesting idea, M/M. You have certainly presented me with an interesting idea."

His insistence on this notion of "interesting" was a sure sign that the fear was not dissipating. Rather, it was becoming more intense. The poor beast was feeling cornered. So much the better.

"I am glad you think so, Professor Hoodwinkle. Would it be possible for me to get those numbers as soon as possible so I can get this meeting arranged?"

It was difficult for me to learn that one should be kind in victory. I felt I was winning this crucial battle.

"I will certainly try, M/M. You must realize, however, that some of these professors, young as they are, may have their phone numbers unlisted. In fact, I have heard it said that one did. Why anyone would want to do that at Ac-Ac U. is beyond me. We are a wonderful family and we are more concerned about the happiness of our faculty than any other institution I know of."

P.H. was beginning to lose it. When he became involved in his own dribble, it was difficult to awaken him. Like quicksand, his own words would begin to slowly swallow his consciousness and he could go on forever with empty platitudes.

"Yes. I am sure that you are completely correct, Professor Hood-winkle. I sense the wonderful family atmosphere at Ac-Ac U. Even though I have only been here a short time. So it does seem strange that anyone would wish to get an unlisted number."

What I did not tell the poor dear (why not turn that one around for a change?) was that my own phone number back at Pholly U. was unlisted. Crank calls from students. What did me in was that weird one during which the caller simply told me that he had picked my number out of the faculty directory. Then he threatened suicide. I was sure that P.H. would somehow never have a phone call like that. These crazy callers must have an instinct that tells them when to stay away from certain less vulnerable people.

"Let me see what I can do, M/M."

P.H.'s parting shot was final. He did not want me to have direct, unmediated access to the women faculty. That was clear. I let him play his games. The essential for me was the meeting itself. To hell with the rest.

What did P.H. do? He arranged for the DULL administrative assistant to get in touch with all parties concerned. And to set up this clearly problematic meeting. After all, I was a member of DULL, and the staff was being as helpful as they could possibly be. My meeting with the women faculty would take place in two weeks, on a Friday night, in my suite at the Guest House.

In Which M/M Attends Her First DULL Faculty Meeting

There it was in my DULL mailbox. (God. I am speaking as if I were really a part of this department!) The notice of the first DULL faculty meeting. Next Thursday afternoon. Thursday afternoons, I came to learn, were a sacred time at DULL. The secretary refused to schedule classes on those afternoons. Faculty were advised to keep them free: no lectures, no office hours, no doctors' appointments. All this out of fear that they might miss a departmental meeting.

The first meeting of the year was more of a general introductory affair. The agenda looked fairly innocuous:

1. Words of welcome from the Chairman
2. Approval of minutes from the last meeting
3. Introduction of new faculty
4. Introduction of new promotees
5. Introduction of guest visitor
6. Statistics on enrollments
7. New business
8. Departmental photo
9. Reception

My first official introduction to the department that was my temporary home!

I arrived at the meeting room five minutes early. P.H., as usual, decided to accompany me. I wondered why he could not trust me to go to a single meeting on my own. Was it that he himself wanted to show off the specimen he had discovered on the beach? Or was it simply that a woman of my rank was such an oddity that she could not be left alone? I would have to make sure that he had no plans to join me when I held my meeting with the women faculty.

So there we were, P.H. and I. Walking into a room that was already filled. Hardly any faces I recognized. DULL prided itself on the variety of areas its course offerings covered. And there before my eyes was the "distinguished" faculty responsible for creating this great variety. P.H. and I sat in two of the very few chairs left open. How unfortunate that these have to be in the front of the room! Just like other gatherings I have attended thus far. I was doomed to that.

4:00 p.m. and still no Professor Assam. I had had the impression that all functions at Ac-Ac U. began right on schedule. I was obviously wrong. 4:05. Assam appears accompanied by Professor Hirsute-du-Vigneron. What a duo! I had forgotten that this was Professor Assam's first meeting as chair and this surely was Hirsute-du-Vigneron's way of endorsing his successor. Hirsute-du-Vigneron sat down among the rest of us while Assam placed himself behind a table that was obviously prepared for the occasion. It was filled with papers that included the agenda of the meeting.

"Welcome one. Welcome all . . ."

Was Assam campaigning for the presidency of Ac-Ac U.? It seemed like déjà vu to me. Did President Schmeergang greet the assembled audience the same way at the Induction Ceremony? I could not for the life of me remember. Too bad. Those words of Schmeergang's were lost forever. Heard and forgotten. I had been unable to take in a pad to that solemn occasion.

"Welcome to what promises to be another great academic year at our distinguished Ac-Ac U. As you all know, this is my first meeting as the new chairman of this distinguished department. My entire being fills with great pride as I look out at the assembled faces and see before me my distinguished predecessors. How grateful I am to them for their effort and their energy in building and maintaining this distinguished department so that it is now one of the university's most distinguished programs. No small feat, my friends."

That last sentence startled me. Being an English professor is a dangerous thing. Especially if one indulges in literary criticism. Why had Assam not placed a "distinguished" in that last sentence? Effect? Clearly, he had decided not to tax his thesaurus. Just as clearly, he was straining to get out the words with the least possible effort. I was impressed. This was certainly better than his performance when I first met him. Perhaps P.H. was right after all and Assam was an extraordinary individual.

The meeting was progressing. Minutes of the last meeting were approved. (One would have to be incredibly anal to retain objections through the summer.) The "distinguished" new members were introduced and asked to stand. Not a woman in the group. One of the new faculty was, however, obviously hand-picked to be the new pride and joy of the department. After his introduction, Assam added that he hoped this new wonder would add to the visibility of the department. After all, was he not taller than all the present faculty?

"Yes," I heard him add, "as Professor Kharaduri"

for that was the name of this genius of a hire...

"walks down the hallways of Ac-Ac U., eyes will not only turn to him but they will look up to him as well. Admirers are bound to speak of our good judgement in managing to seduce this new colleague to Ac-Ac U."

As for the promotees, they were, of course, all men. I should not have been surprised. Had I not after all attended the Induction Ceremony? There they were: the Professors-ès-Groin and the Belly Button Professors. Attired in their new ties. And surprise of surprises the ties impeccably reached the appropriate body part. Look at me, they seemed to be saying. Without an exception the promotees all had shit-eating grins. I somehow knew that President Arnoldo Salvatore Schmeergang would be beaming with pride at his new academic children. The promotees did not look terribly familiar to me. But then again I had been waylaid at the ceremony by Schmeergang himself and did not have the chance to meet many of the Induction goers. DULL had outperformed its competition with two new promotees in each rank. What a great future this promised for the younger faculty in the department!

I glanced at the agenda quickly. I was next. Assam introduced P.H. who then did me the honors. I was fading in and out.

"... distinguished visitor ... fell from space ... Ha! Ha! ... please welcome her to your distinguished department."

How familiar everyone's words were becoming! This time, fortunately, I did not have to give a speech. I merely had to stand and allow the assembled multitudes a chance to gape at this strange visitor.

No sooner had I sat down than the administrative assistant began distributing the statistics on enrollments. Over my extended visit, I would come to discover that charts and computer lay-outs were Assam's specialty. He loved to devise new ways of setting out the information at his disposal. Faculty salaries. Course numbers. Supply budget. His deft hands entered and charted it all.

New business. Always my favorite part of any departmental meeting. One could never tell what people would come up with. And, here, I was not to be disappointed. A professor stood up. (One had to stand up before speaking so that the audience could see the length of the tie.) He was a Groin Tie. His bright red hair reminded me of Woody Woodpecker.

"There is a grave matter about which I am concerned, Professor Assam. I hope you will allow me to bring it up. And since this is only the first departmental meeting of the year, perhaps the matter can be resolved, unlike others I have raised, before the end of the first semester."

What could Assam say? I could read impatience in his eyes. He himself was reading the Groin Tie's lips.

"As you know, I have some very highly placed friends and colleagues on the international political scene."

I knew the genre to which this Groin Tie belonged. Full of himself. Yet insecure. Trying to impress his listeners. Yet afraid he is not doing it fast enough. This boded ill for a speedy conclusion to an otherwise painless meeting.

"These colleagues do come to visit me in my office. There are two interrelated things that concern me deeply: the vending machine and the cleaning supplies."

The vending machine? What the hell was this GT talking about?

"Let me tackle the vending machine first. As you know, the vending machine for the entire building is next to my office. It is unsightly and demeaning for a department of the stature of DULL to have this enormously garish machine gracing the office door of one of its most distinguished faculty. As one approaches my office, one hears nothing but the sound of money making its way into the belly of the machine. Clang. Clang. Clang. And here I am, a distinguished Professor-ès-Groin in a distinguished department, trying to carry on a learned discussion with a visiting dignitary.

"To add insult to injury, the machine is placed in such a way that it invariably has crowds of students gathered around it. As if the entrance to my office were some kind of bar. Really! And can you imagine what it is like for me to teach a seminar in this building and have the students slurping the entire time? Slurp. Slurp. Slurp. If they had no access to the machine, they would not avail themselves of these liquids. Digesting them instead of my ideas. Really.

"I assure you that should another university offer me a position, the presence of a vending machine near my office will be a decisive factor in my decision. It would be ill-advised for DULL to pit its faculty against a tawdry clanking vending machine.

"I am quite aware that several colleagues find the presence of this machine as deeply disturbing as I do. But they do not have my courage. I beg of you, sir, to speak to the Ac-Ac U. administration about this problem. So much for the vending machine."

I was watching Assam. He looked furious. His face was changing color. I could tell he did not want to respond. Worse still for him was to have the department's dirty laundry aired in front of a visiting dignitary (that is, after all, what I am, dear ones). P.H. was equally upset. He was showing his characteristic twitch. Meaning he was quite beyond himself.

But this pain-in-the-ass Professor-ès-Groin—who did not seem to suffer from an excess of modesty—had other stories to tell.

"I realize I am bringing up these things rather unexpectedly."

"You sure are, you little bastard." I think I almost heard Assam say this.

"BUT the problem of the cleaning supplies cannot continue. Their presence in the hallways of the department is inexcusable. Mops. Cleaning fluids. Pails. I repeat: Inexcusable. There I was two weeks ago deep in conversation with a student about an issue raised in class. You can well imagine that I was distracted. The damn cleaning woman had left the supplies in the hallway next to my office door. Probably after buying a drink from that infernal vending machine. Right into the pail I went. How embarrassing for a man of my academic distinction!"

The audience was controlling itself. Most of Groin Tie's listeners were on the edge of laughter. I was picturing, as the rest of the DULL faculty was, this Professor-ès-Groin with his tie in the cleaning pail. Rather unsightly for someone of his stature.

"I beseech you, Professor Assam. This is a serious problem indeed."

With this, the Groin Tie seated himself once more. I could not tell which problem was the more serious for him: the cleaning fluids or the drinking fluids. He had very effectively pecked at Assam, whose face had progressively turned red, a red that did not quite match that of the Groin Tie's hair. I quickly began to beg the forgiveness of all woodpeckers for my initial comparison. Why did my poor animal friends have to be mentioned in the context of the Ac-Ac U. Groin Ties?

Assam thanked Professor Bruttorio (that was the name of the Groin Tie) for his eloquent and impassioned plea. He promised to look into the problem. Good luck, I wanted to tell Assam. If he did not look into it, I was certain that Professor Bruttorio would remind him.

Time for the picture! This was a departmental ritual that took place after every first meeting of the year. Rows and rows of smiling faces clumped together populated the chair's office. They were part of the unchanging wall furniture, lovingly handed down from one authority figure to another.

I, M/M, as the visiting guest of the department simply had to be in the picture. Object as I might, I could not convince my dear male colleagues that I should not be permanently the only female in their departmental photographic exhibit. So there I was in the front row, flanked on one side by the outgoing chair of DULL, Professor Hirsute-du-Vigneron, and on the other by the present chair, Professor Assam. Standing behind me was P.H. Beaming proudly. As if he were offering me on a silver platter. Click. Click. Click. And, thank God, it was over.

Time for the reception. P.H. cornered me on the spot. He was obviously still upset about Bruttorio's performance, because he began immediately to excuse him.

"You know, M/M, life for Professor Arturo Bruttorio has not been easy."

"Is it for anyone, Professor Hoodwinkle?"

"Right you are. But his especially has been an immense disappointment. He was inducted into the Order of the Cravates relatively late in his career. His ambitions, I am afraid, have been greater than his production. He has been desperately trying to be chairman of DULL, but without success. Much of the department despises him.

"You see, M/M, he also predicted the demise of the department. A silly act. Of course, this department is strong and healthy. Demise? At the time, I advised him that this was not a sound prediction. And it did not come about. Bruttorio was quite distraught. He started talking to himself. He started walking around reciting medieval verse. He stopped greeting people when he saw them in the hallway. He stopped cutting his hair on a regular basis. His long red hair dangled miserably over his entire head. A pity. A pity, I assure you.

"He also has the reputation, poor man, and I think unfairly mind you, of terrorizing the students and the faculty."

"Where is his office?" I asked.

"First door on your left."

How wrong you are, P.H., I wanted to add. Why not say it, M/M?

"You know, Professor Hoodwinkle, this reputation for terrorizing students and colleagues may not be as unfair as you think. I remember walking by that office door only yesterday and hearing screaming coming from Bruttorio's office."

"That is quite impossible, M/M."

"Why is it so impossible? My ears do not deceive me, I assure you. It was screaming I heard. In fact, I was so concerned that I asked the staff at the departmental office. They did not seem at all shocked. One secretary even assured me that this was by no means unusual.

Professor Hoodwinkle, I have never liked bullies. Much less academic bullies."

"Oh. No. M/M. I am certain that you misunderstood the staff. I assure you of that. What you heard from behind Professor Bruttorio's door were dramatic readings."

(*Dramatic readings, my ass, I wanted to say. But instead what came out was*):

"Oh. By the way, how did Professor Arturo Bruttorio get this far?"

"Well, M/M. This is a very important question. One, I should add, that most colleagues do not ask. I know the answer only because I served on the dean's promotion committee when Arturo came up for promotion to the rank of Professor-ès-Groin. Between you and me, M/M, Arturo's work has been greatly misunderstood. He has had to publish his books in his own press in the basement of his house. But, since you will have a chance to observe the promotion process first hand, you will see why we all agreed that Arturo's file was indeed outstanding. His measure was the highest."

I was not convinced that P.H.'s logic was the best. I would see how the promotion committee worked soon enough. For now, it was time to meet some of my cherished colleagues!

Circulating at receptions was not my forte. Here, however, I did not have much to worry about. Once again, I was the star attraction. A woman full professor. Male bodies milled around me. I had not met any of the faculty first hand. They only existed for me as names and biographies on the faculty list. Now I could feast my eyes on them.

P.H. was being incredibly helpful. Identifying the major personalities.

"There is Professor Flysmudge."

A roly-poly Groin Tie walked in front of me. He was the senior professor in the department and had helped found DULL. He apparently always wore a satisfied smile. The kind that comes from thinking you are the best. The kind that men tend to have more than women. He was dressed in a pair of light brown polyester pants worn high over his protruding belly. A tucked in tee shirt showed his physique badly—quite badly. The tee shirt-polyester pants combo had a garnish that gave the entirety that special touch of DULL elegance: Flysmudge's initials on the breast pocket of his tee shirt. T.F. Thurber Flysmudge. This was only visible from the front of this mass of flesh that was one of the distinguished founders of DULL. And his Groin Tie? It hung limply over the tee shirt, as though it were asking: what am I doing in this outrageous outfit?

I was introduced to Professor Flysmudge, who might, as P.H. promised, have some interesting tidbits on the history of his home department.

"It is very nice to meet you, M/M. You are probably wondering about my name. I realize that it is rather unorthodox and believe me I have been subjected to many a joke about it. But can you deny your paternity? Or your maternity, for you feminists? Ha! Ha!"

Flysmudge was certainly pleased with his verbal skills. P.H. had already warned me about his sensitivity to his name. He even had a plaque inscribed with what came to be known lovingly in DULL as the "No Swat Motto." "I Never Kill Flies," was Flysmudge's motto. His name was only a secondary reason for this decision. Professor Flysmudge had lived extensively in non-Western countries with large fly populations, and being an animal lover, he simply abhorred the treatment the fly received worldwide. He had at times even thought of writing a scholarly study on this most unjust of human behaviors but was awaiting an opportune moment for it.

P.H. was a wealth of information. I wondered if he had any idea of the deep distaste he created in me when he went on with these stories. But, after all, were he to stop, would I be able to even write about my experience at Ac-Ac U.?

I was looking around. Trying to get my bearings in this august company. All of a sudden, a booming voice accosted me.

"I have been looking forward to meeting you, M/M. I am Professor Gerhard Schnoozeheit."

"Hello. I am quite pleased to meet you too, Professor Schnoozeheit. But, correct me if I am wrong, you are only an adjunct member of DULL, isn't that so?"

"Absolutely correct. My research, as you know, actually places me squarely in DULL's major areas of interest. Like my work on mouths."

"Mouths."

"Oh, yes. Absolutely fascinating. If you would honor me with a few minutes of your time, I will be more than happy to explain all this to you."

I was tempted for one brief moment to reject this kind offer. Fortunately, I thought better of it—and quickly.

"Yes. Of course."

"It is like this, my dear." (*Oh, no. Not this one too!*) "You may have heard of my book, *Big Mouths*. If I may be so immodest, I can honestly say that the work broke new ground. It deals with the speed with which one opens one's mouth when uttering certain words. Mind you,

I was quite interested in the cultural variants of this phenomenon around the world."

"Tell me, my dear Professor Schnoozeheit, what difference is there between languages?"

I watched his face change color as the words "my dear" penetrated his thick skull. Would he be able to answer me? Sure enough, his desire to brag about his work took over.

"Difference in languages? Hm . . . Hm . . . What a wonderful idea! It never occurred to me. Can you imagine?"

Yes, I was tempted to say, I certainly can imagine. How many of our own distinguished types at Pholly U. prided themselves on their unsound scholarship.

"You see, I have traveled all over the globe carrying my stopwatch. I have braved social occasions. I have braved meetings. I have even been punched out a few times by individuals who thought I had come a bit too close to their mouths for comfort."

That certainly awoke me. I had to suppress a laugh. Thinking about this old Groin Tie being hit for invading people's space with his stopwatch. What a way to put someone off! This guy would really have to be watched. I found myself moving slowly away from Professor Schnoozeheit. I was waiting for him to pop out his damn stopwatch. He must have spotted my nervousness because he assured me that that phase of his research was over. What was he involved in now?

"Business secret, M/M. Ha! Ha! You know, I am usually reluctant to discuss my work. It is so original and breaks such important new ground that I am afraid to reveal it to anyone."

Certainly, Professor Schnoozeheit did not suffer from modesty.

"You will be one of the privileged few fortunate enough to hear about my latest research. That is only—you understand—because you are a visitor to Ac-Ac U. and I trust that you will not disclose any of this to anyone."

"Trust me, Professor Schnoozeheit." I was quick to reply. "The secret will go no further than this room."

After all, I assumed that Professor Schnoozeheit would never have the occasion to read the account of my adventures at Ac-Ac U.

"You see, this work on the speed of mouth-openings led me down the path of the body. And active body research is, of course, very sensitive. So what could I do? I thought long and hard about it. You will never guess what I am now involved in. Informal surveys on the use of deodorants."

"Deodorants?"

"Yes. It is a very important cultural question. How do people use it? Do they prefer the roll-on or the spray? I try to ask colleagues and friends casually. After my experience with the mouth research, I must admit that I have not dared approach strangers on the street about their deodorant preference."

"How is this informal research going?"

"Extremely well. I have almost completed the work. You know, I was approached by several deodorant manufacturers who must have somehow heard about my research."

I was sure I knew how these companies had heard about Schnoozeheit's research. The alacrity with which he opened up to me was not unusual for him, I suspected.

"These manufacturers were ready to pay handsomely for my results, informal though they might be. I would certainly not be here today had I accepted their generous offers. But, I was trained in the highest ideals of research. My work, I feel, is answering important cultural questions. You have noticed, M/M, haven't you, that people smell different?"

I was sure that Professor Schnoozeheit was not looking for an answer from me. How would one reply to this fossil's questions? From the mouth to the armpit! What a trajectory!

This was apparently Schnoozeheit's major project since the one on the mouths. He had gone through a bad period when the wells had been dry. Why?

"Academic politics. What else, M/M? I am only now waking from my academic sleep. My friends refer to me lovingly as the Rip van Winkle of Ac-Ac U."

"Well, Professor Schnoozeheit. Where will you go after this?"

"Wonderful question, M/M. I should admit to you that there is a project close to my heart: snoring through the ages. I have been collecting material over the years from different sources: literary, philosophical, and so on."

"Are you familiar with Professor Somnanbule's course?"

"Yes, of course, my dear." (*Not again. Not again. I am going to tear my hair out.*) "We are very close friends. Very close, indeed. We have not slept together. Ha! Ha! But we have shared ideas and more."

I had not yet become used to the Ac-Ac U. sense of humor. I was having trouble keeping my attention on what Schnoozeheit was saying. As so often happens with me, I found my eyes roaming around the room. A sure sign that I should change the scenery.

"Thank you so much, Professor Schnoozeheit, for your time. But I must really leave."

With this, I escaped from the DULL reception. Fortunately, the DULLards and their guests were so involved in receiving one another that they did not even notice my departure. I was not anxious to have another pre-exit run-in with P.H.

In Which M/M Introduces S. P.-T. Directly to the Intellectual Life of DULL

I literally ran home. I had once again left S. P.-T. alone for the entire day. Something I did not much like doing. But this time, I had a special present for her.

S. P.-T. She was not overly pleased with the Guest House. But more traumatic for her was the litter situation. The absence of animal companions at Ac-Ac U. proved to be more of a problem than I had anticipated. Where would S. P.-T. perform her bodily functions? I was inspired by a particularly miserly colleague at Pholly U. He did not buy cat litter for his cat but himself shredded newspaper into a make-shift container. He replaced the newspaper on a daily basis.

So there I was in this alien environment trying to be creative. Box covers were the solution. How fortunate for me that the DULL meeting was today! And how even more appropriate! I had walked into the office and asked the secretary for a box cover. I did not reveal to her the reason for my need. She simply motioned me to the supply closet and handed me the key. I walked in and turned on the light. Lo and behold! What should stare at me but a box cover with Thurber Flysmudge's name. I grabbed it. I learned that it had been part of a now defunct box that once held the papers from a volume in honor of Flysmudge, edited by none other than Hirsute-du-Vigneron and Assam. Now the box cover would serve a more noble purpose. It would turn into a container in which S. P.-T. could defecate to her heart's content.

My entrance into our quarters elicited a great vocal welcome from my friend and companion. It was as if she knew what I had in store for her. Rather than simply listening to my stories about DULL, she could now be a direct participant in the DULL experience.

In Which M/M Finally Meets the Women Faculty of Ac-Ac U.

I do not think that I have ever seen an event be so important to so many people. Everyone at Ac-Ac U. was abuzz with information about my impending meeting with the women faculty. It was as if there were some conspiracy between us to do something illegal. This was to be nothing but an innocent meeting. Male eyes watched me anxiously for days before the by-now infamous meeting. What would I tell my female colleagues? What would they tell me?

My first major shouting match with P.H. I did not know the old geezer had it in him. There he is trying to convince me that he should attend what he calls the "women's meeting." This is a get together, I tell him. I feel the need to talk to some of my own gender. To exchange ideas. To share feelings. I do not want a man invading this space. P.H. will simply not take no for an answer. The Guest House is on university property. I must adhere to university regulations. That is all right. I argue back. The women can meet in a coffee shop.

"A coffee shop? How could you even suggest such a horrible idea, M/M? At least in your suite, no one will see you."

I could see that P.H. was really torn up over this. Should he crash the "women's meeting" in my closed quarters? Or, should he risk having these women meeting in a public space and maybe exposing the university to unnecessary negative publicity? His weakness would allow me to really push him.

"All right, Professor Hoodwinkle. The meeting will take place in my Guest House. That is after all what we told our colleagues, is it not? But I must insist that you not attend. Frankly, should you appear for this meeting, I will simply not let you enter."

His face was turning all sorts of colors before my eyes. I was sure no one had ever dared speak to him like this. To challenge his authority. And a woman, no less? I wondered for a moment if he would quit in a huff. No. The visitor was much too important to him. Clearly, his own status at Ac-Ac U. had been improved by his discovery of the female alien. Rising academic stock. Had he been given directions from the upper administration to act as spy for this gathering? It would not surprise me. If so, the male honchos were in for a disappointment.

"You certainly feel strongly about this, M/M. I will respect your wishes."

Friday evening. I am relieved that P.H. will not make an appearance at my door. Because that is exactly how far he would have gotten.

The doorbell rings. Voices are outside. I let them in. The five women faculty at the entirety of Ac-Ac U. How young they look! They obviously know one another and decided to come all together. Strength in numbers? I cannot help but wonder if they do all their outings as a group.

"Come on in. Come on in. I am M/M."

I hug them as they enter my suite. S. P.-T. is watching the proceedings. Effusive greetings are not new to her. I introduce her to the guests.

They are nervous. I offer them seats and they take them. The wine and cheese have already been set out. I serve them and I myself sit down.

"Thank you very much for the invitation, M/M."

The sentence emanates from a blond-haired woman dressed in a suit. The others are watching her. She has clearly taken on the role of group leader. This makes me uncomfortable.

"We are very honored to have this opportunity of meeting you. But you understand, we are sure, our very sensitive position at Ac-Ac U. We have decided, as a group, not to reveal our names."

I am even more uncomfortable now. I realize these women faculty have chosen a strategy. One based on fear and respect of the male administrative power structure. This will never do. I would not have been surprised to learn that the chairs of their departments had gotten to them somehow. Prior to the meeting. Threatening them? Telling them their futures would be jeopardized by talking to me? I had seen plenty of this in my ten years at Pholly U. I myself had been accused of talking to junior faculty who were friends about departmental problems. If they are foolish to think that they are in Paradise, one must not dissuade them from that idea. I will never forget that one meeting with my chair, whose name has fortunately been erased from my memory bank, in which he accused me of corrupting the academic morals of his junior faculty. This is most likely what the Ac-Ac U. administration was afraid of. So they had simply transferred their own fear onto these women.

"Yes. I do realize how difficult this is for all of you. Believe me."

I can tell by the looks in their eyes that they are a bit skeptical. They have probably all written their dissertations under male supervision. If one had a problem, she assumed it was her own unique situation that generated it. Other problems along the way will have been largely forgotten by now. Only an emotional deep probe would unearth them. They will also have convinced themselves that they are the exception to the rule of gender. That they are the women who will be accepted by the male Ac-Ac U. establishment. I wanted to scream out that I went down this path too. That I also thought, fool that I was, that I would be accepted as a real scholar in the community of male scholars. But screaming would not get me anywhere here. That I knew.

Perhaps the issue was not so simple for them. Perhaps my being a full professor was enough to convince them that I was in the enemy camp. After all, was I not in the constant company of Professor Hood-winkle? In setting up this wine and cheese meeting, I had not bargained for all this.

"I am very flattered that you have all accepted my invitation. I was curious about life for a woman academic in this world that is clearly all male. I understand your desire to keep your identity secret but how should I address you?"

"Don't worry. We have thought of all that. We have taken the alphabet and assigned the first five letters, a letter to each of us, in the order of our birth dates. The oldest is A, the second oldest is B, and so on. I am A."

This was the one who spoke earlier. Was this her idea? She then proceeded to introduce B, C, D, and E. I tried to attach some kind of personal physical characteristic to each of the letters so that I could remember who was who. B was also blond-haired, so B made sense to me. Her hair was longer than A's. So far so good. C was a redhead with a charming smile. D was dark-haired. That left E. How odd that she should be the most elegant of the group. I frankly found her dress inappropriate for a woman academic: a short white skirt with a white matching skimpy jacket. Under the jacket was a sheer—quite sheer, in fact—black shirt through which one could see E's black bra and some cleavage. Topping the entire outfit were long red-painted nails. I was sure that she made the Groin Ties faint with desire.

C piped up. "We are very pleased to be here. You must not make too much of the fact that we are so cautious. Most of us have not had an easy time of it here and we have become quite touchy."

I was not sure how to proceed. This meeting was not running according to plan. I expected a gregarious group. One that would be talking all at once. One in which stories would be told. One in which ideas would be exchanged. One in which joy and laughter would dominate. This had been my experience at the majority of women's meetings I had attended at Pholly U. and elsewhere.

"I understand that you write poetry." This was D. A soft voice, unassuming.

"Yes, I do, D."

"Would you mind reading some to us?" Her reply was quick.

"I do not normally like to read my poetry. I write it for my own edification. A sort of exorcism of life's situations, if you wish."

"That is quite all right," responded D. "None of us is a poetry specialist. It might be inspirational."

I really hated to read my poetry in public. Writing it was a very personal and private act. But if I myself was not willing to open up to these women faculty, how could I expect them to do so for me? Then there was the problem of what poem to choose. How would they respond to it? I decided to take my chances.

"On one condition. That no one comment on my poems. Are we in agreement?"

"Yes," their voices sang out in unison.

My voice rang out:

> A woman walks down the street.
> Black and blue.
> Tell-tale signs.
> Signs of battering . . .
> Visible.
>
> A woman walks down the street.
> No visible signs.
> A battered woman nevertheless.
>
> Who is the deity who dictates
>   that battering is only
>   physical?
> Who is the deity who dictates
>   the superiority of the
>   visible?
>
> Battered.
> Battered.

Battered.
I have been raped and battered.

No.
I cannot go to a hospital.
No.
I cannot have my body examined.
Their semen will not appear on any slides . . .
Nor will their excrement.

Their assaults are not physical.

Words.
Words.
Words.
Their verbal cannons invade my emotional being.

Horrific beasts that consume what crosses their path.
Vermin that invade what crosses their path.

Bruised is my existence.
Externally whole.
Internally mangled.
What does one do with beasts?
What does one do with vermin?
A ritual ablution?
A daily cleansing?

Lady Macbeth had no perfumes of Araby.
Neither do I.

Words.
Let words exorcise words.
Vomit the verbal poison.
And spit it at them.
Take different words . . . and create.

From wounds, create . . .
Turn the pus of dead wounds
        into life-giving liquids.
And come forth, rejuvenated.

The silence of the end of my poem was greeted by a mirror silence on the part of my audience. I was watching the entire group. Especially E. Was her dress a reflection of her attitude to women in the workplace? I thought I had seen her flinch a bit while I was reciting.

The wine was flowing. The cheese was disappearing. My new-found friends were beginning to relax.

"I know about our pre-reading agreement. But I would like to ask one question: Is the poem autobiographical?" This was B. Gutsy.

"Everything I write is autobiographical. Even my criticism has autobiographical components. Don't you find that to be the case, B?"

"I have never really thought about it, M/M. Certainly my own graduate training in Comparative Studies never quite made me think about these issues. But once you mention it, it seems only natural that everything we write should have us in it."

I felt encouraged by B's response. She was actually talking about herself. The others were still a bit taciturn. I offered more wine. Two bottles later, we had all mellowed. I was even hearing some laughter.

In Which M/M Is Treated to Some Great Stories

A was in really great form. What a storyteller!

"Do you remember the time that Flysmudge fainted?"

"Flysmudge? Of DULL fame?" I responded.

"Yes."

We were all giggling. The name itself. I had been struck by it when I first met the great man himself at the DULL reception. But, here, among us women, it seemed even more ridiculous. We all begged A to tell the story.

"Once upon a time, there was a Thurber Flysmudge. Blessed with a great tee shirt . . ."

Laughter was beginning to resound.

". . . and a name guaranteed to entertain those who met him. One thing in his favor: he was able to laugh at himself. Word has it that in the old days, he would come up to newcomers at Ac-Ac U. and buzz like a fly."

I had trouble containing myself. Imagining the blubber that was Flysmudge buzzing at the young Ac-Acers. I burst out in laughter. The rest joined me fast enough.

"One day, Flysmudge fainted in class. How fortunate that the class was being held in the DULL seminar room. Professor Hirsute-du-Vigneron was still the chair."

I was pleased that A did not say chairman—progress there was.

"He rushed out, shirt sticking out of his pants, belly showing."

More laughter. Us girls simply had no respect.

"He had the secretary call for an ambulance. What a job that emergency crew had lifting Flysmudge off the floor! One of them was even overheard saying: 'Why don't this guy weigh some'in closer to his name? Sure would be a hell of a lot easier to lift if he was as light as a fly! My luck to land the fat slob!' But, that was his job. And he did it.

"Flysmudge was taken to the hospital and attended by the best physicians. He had begun to talk nonsense and ask silly questions. What year was he in? Was Professor Hirsute-du-Vigneron still the chairman (sorry about that M/M but I am using his words here) of DULL? So he was sent to a psychiatrist. The psychiatrist was at once impressed and dismayed by Flysmudge's attitude. After all, here was a distinguished professor from an even more distinguished university. And he was talking nonsense? So he ordered a bank of tests.

"You should have been here for that, M/M. It would have given you enough to muse about for the rest of your life. The test results were whispered in the corridors. People talked about them at the Faculty Club. Had we all been Catholics, we would not have stopped crossing ourselves."

"Go on, A." We all said it at once.

"The test results? Flysmudge was brain-dead and had been for years."

"No."

A loud boom. Female voices echoed in my Guest House. S. P.-T., who had been watching us with semi-closed eyes, head on her outstretched paws, even lifted that cute head of hers a bit and began moving one of her ears in that characteristic radar-like action, as if to ask what we were up to.

"Yes. Brain-dead. This explained the unreturned blue books. This explained the unchanging syllabi. They all made sense now. Even Hirsute-du-Vigneron had to admit that he had been hearing complaints from students for years about these problems. But he had shrugged them off."

"My God. I simply cannot believe this."

"Oh, yes, M/M. Incredible as it seems, it was medically verified. The administration doubted the medical findings. So the poor physicians had to repeat their tests. No doubt about it. One could see the worried looks on the faces of the big muck-mucks. Should Flysmudge be eased out? Their hands were tied. He was already tenured. And besides he looked right: gray hair, gray beard. So why not keep him on? After all, had he not functioned beautifully for all these years? Everyone now spoke of 'all these years' because no one could pin down the exact moment at which Flysmudge's brain had tuned out. DULL—and everyone else I might add—was given strict instructions: not a word to the students, lest it leak out to other authorities.

"So there we are. From fainting spell to administrative cover-up. The fallout? Everyone—I must admit I myself was guilty of this— began looking at the older members of the faculty. What about them?

Were they brain-dead? Did they qualify for the Flysmudge syndrome? Every time a rotund gray-haired Groin Tie smiled at me, I wondered if he belonged in a nursing home rather than a university."

A seemed to really know the ins and outs of DULL. What a savvy politician. I complimented her on her skills. This was her third year at Ac-Ac U., she admitted, and she made it her business to know what was going on. For a woman, this was not an altogether easy business.

A's story made us all conscious of an unspoken bond. Hugs of good-byes. We agreed that we would have more of these wine and cheese gatherings and where possible more poetry by other than yours truly would be read.

The names? I had actually over the evening grown fond of the letters. For me, the women faculty became personalized through their initials.

In Which M/M Becomes a Member of COOC

Monday morning. My meeting with the women faculty had rejuvenated me. So off I went to DULL. And there in my mailbox was a personal letter from Arnoldo Salvatore Schmeergang. How pleased he was to have met me, what an honor, etc. All right, I was tempted to say, let us cut the crap. What is the bottom line, Arnoldo? Well, the dear president of Ac-Ac U. was cashing in his chips. Calling on my great expertise and knowledge, etc. He was appointing me member of the Committee to Oversee the Order of the Cravates, COOC. He hoped I would agree to serve on this important committee. Would I please call his office with my decision as soon as possible so that a meeting could be scheduled right away?

What an opportunity! This was better than I had hoped! To give my feedback on the entire business with the ties! I picked up the phone and dialed Schmeergang's office. His secretary was most anxious to hear from me. The meeting was being scheduled with my convenience in mind. Tomorrow? Why not?

In Which M/M Gets Introduced to the COOC

There I was in the Presidential Seminar Room in Ac-Ac U.'s main administrative building. A room that belonged, in effect, to Schmeergang. He alone could schedule meetings in it. Not even his administrative assistant had a say in that. The faces of the other COOC members expressed the great respect and admiration they felt at even being allowed into the room. Wood paneling. Velvet curtains. A rectangular mahogany table. Plush soft chairs. The entirety being blessed by framed pictures of past Ac-Ac U. presidents, looking down at the committee members from their height on the wall. All wore dark suits. All wore bow ties. All smiled with great confidence and paternalism.

The COOC members were invited to sit down. We had not been told in advance who our committee co-members were. There was P.H. smiling at me. Why should I have been surprised to see him? I could see that nothing was done at Ac-Ac U. without his presence. And to his right, like a docile dog, was Professor Assam. An agenda was placed in front of every chair. President Schmeergang sat at the head of the table, beaming. His thick round designer glasses could not even begin to dream of hiding the glint in his eyes. Definitely a big moment in Ac-Ac U. history.

"Dear friends and colleagues," Schmeergang began. "I am very pleased to welcome you on the Committee to Oversee the Order of the Cravates. This is a new committee I have set up on my own authority. I did not even consult the Committee on Committees. And, believe me, I did not do this lightly.

"But we are in a period of transition here at Ac-Ac U. The face of academia is changing."

(*What? A progressive president? Let us see how far he is willing to go!*)

"We have, as you know, been hiring women faculty for the past few years and we are facing a dilemma with the Order of the Cravates. So I have asked you here to discuss various important topics relating to women and ties. Other issues that come to your mind will also be welcome.

"Let me, however, begin by introducing the members of this distinguished"

(*again??*)

"committee. I have purposefully kept the number small, only
five of you, with myself as chair. This will allow for better and more
useful interaction and decision-making. I have also chosen the members very carefully to reflect different perspectives, yet not so different
that we cannot come to a resolution after our deliberations."

Schmeergang started to move around the table. I was, needless to
say, the only female. I had already noticed on entering the room that
all my other "distinguished" colleagues were Groin Ties. This was
clearly a most important committee! There was P.H. There was Professor Assam. There was Professor Schnoozeheit. I thought I remembered
meeting that face! Now I understood why he persisted in maintaining
that shit-eating grin directed at me. There I was.

But then who should be presented but Professor Alphonse Le
Pneu. He needed no introduction. My ears had already been filled
with his marvelous talents and his wondrous acts. And all this despite
the fact that he had nothing to do with my home department, DULL.
Every time I heard P.H. talk about him—a treat I received on repeated
occasions—I felt I had to flush out my head. He was the administration's favored son. Everything he touched turned to gold. I have
always been fascinated by these phenomena. Certainly they were not
an unfamiliar occurrence at Pholly U. How do these males get chosen?
Is it their dress? Is it their demeanor? The upper administration's attitude to them was always one of total fascination and enchantment.
Almost quasi-sexual in its nature.

I had fortunately forgotten the name of Le Pneu's parallel at
Pholly U. Let us just call him X. I remember running into the dean of
the College at the Faculty Club when I was by necessity forced to have
lunch there (I normally avoided it like the plague). X had invited him
to lunch without an obvious reason. There was our own "distinguished" dean, looking around nervously. When he did not spot X, he
panicked. What choice did he have but to address me? Was I going to
X's luncheon? No. In fact, I had no idea what the hell he was talking
about. I was taking the staff of my department out to lunch. And since
I was not a member of the Club, one of the staff had kindly lent me her
membership number and I was paying her back. She admired the
dean, so I invited him to join us. He looked quite upset. Like a teenager
in love. Woe of woes, he had been stood up by X. But eat with the staff?
Not on your life. Holding his head down like an abandoned puppy, he
proceeded to go through the buffet line.

So this was Le Pneu. I took a good look at him. To say that I was taken aback by his appearance would be an understatement. A shocking head of bright blond hair mixed with gray surrounded his deeply tanned face. The ensemble looked a bit like a whitewall tire. He looked like he spent much of his time in the sun. Certainly, he had not been frequenting his study. But then he probably did not need to. Being a favorite at the academic court would forgive many an absence in one's publishing record. Would he be different from X? When the latter spat, the administration was there in a split second with its spittoon. I promised myself that I would watch Professor Le Pneu very closely on this committee.

In Which M/M Listens to Some Tie History

President Arnoldo Salvatore Schmeergang, with the wisdom inherent in his venerable office, decided to begin the meeting with a brief history of the Order of the Cravates at Ac-Ac U. The hierarchy came first in Schmeergang's presentation: as far back as one could document, only the president of Ac-Ac U. wore a bow tie. This singular privilege brought with it great variety. Colors were permitted. Like a peacock, the president of Ac-Ac U., no matter who he was, was free to display his plumage.

Now that we all obviously understood who was on top, Schmeergang relaxed. The problem was with the ties. The Order of the Cravates was a singular feature that Ac-Ac U. shared with no other institution. Time was when there were three ranks: the CT, the BT, and the GT.

The Chest Tie signaled the junior faculty. The untenured lot. Those whose future at Ac-Ac U. was not assured. The CT had, however, been eliminated in the past few years with the hiring of the women faculty. And this was part of the reason I, M/M, was here. At least according to Schmeergang. To help in the deliberations on the future of the Order with the influx of new academic blood. The demise of so fine a tradition as the Chest Tie was not an easy matter, President Schmeergang confessed. At the time, it was without doubt the easiest solution, he added.

"Fortunately, we do not have any tenured women."

I inadvertently moved. If looks could kill, I am sure mine would have. A direct shot at President Schmeergang. He was smart, however. He quickly figured out that it had been an impolitic thing to say.

"Sorry, M/M. I mean not yet."

Yeah, right. I was tempted to say.

He continued. Since no women had come up for promotion yet, the BT and the GT traditions had been kept. One point had been raised at the time of the elimination of the CTs. Did BT stand for Belt Tie or

Belly Button Tie? A.S.S. (the initials seemed more fitting after his last blunder) appointed a committee to look into the various options and possibilities. To Belt or to Belly Button. That was the question.

"Those of you who were not privileged to have been Groin Ties at the time had not become aware of this controversy. The committee found its task extremely difficult. But what an astute group of people! I read their report. It was one of my proudest moments! I knew then that I had appointed the right individuals. What a feeling, I must admit. And, as you all know, they opted for Belly Button. Their logic was inescapable. The Chest Tie, though it had been discontinued, was gauged on a part of the body. Likewise with the Groin Tie. Was it not proper then for the BT to refer to an anatomical part and not to a piece of clothing? Hence: the Belly Button Tie."

What logic! I was watching my dear committee co-members. They all looked overwhelmed with emotion. Ah! The glory and the pride that come with tradition!

In Which M/M Tells the COOCs the Significance of Ties

A.S.S. was going on. Clearly, nothing could stop him.

"The challenge is before us. Women will join our faculty in increasing numbers. What are we to do? What do you think M/M?"

Did Schmeergang really want my response? No matter. I will give it.

"You know, President Schmeergang, this issue is quite complicated. Before I direct myself to your specific concerns, might I be permitted to give you my theory on ties? It will at least help you and the COOC understand any later ideas I might have."

"Please, M/M. Go ahead."

"I have for many years been fascinated by the tie as social and cultural phenomenon. Why is it of all male dress the item that gets imported least to women? Sure, we see women once in a while wearing ties. Sure, there are some foolhardy designers who will propose this item for a feminine market. But, notice, gentlemen, that this vestimentary item has never taken off with the female population. Unlike pants, to take one example. Unlike vests, to take another.

"Why is this? Clearly, there are deeper cultural reasons for the instability of ties among women. Gentlemen, the tie is a stand-in for the male sexual organ!"

I was watching my male audience. My words produced a greater impact than if I had told them I had a gun and was preparing to murder them all, one after the other. Shock. Fear. Mouths open, they stared at me.

"Yes, gentlemen. The tie is a surrogate penis."

I must admit I was enjoying this. Shocking them. Frightening them. My male colleagues had done it to me often enough over my ten years at Pholly U. Damn the COOC of Ac-Ac U. Let its members pay the price.

"Why else would a tie hang from a man's neck the way his sexual organ hangs from his body? Let us be grateful, gentlemen, for the inventor of the tie. After all, what would you all have done had he (for I firmly believe it was a 'he') decided to starch the tie and prop it from the shirt in a fully erect position?"

Speechlessness was the only response my words produced. I decided to continue.

"Do not kid yourselves, my dears. The male is no different from the female. He also likes to parade in public with a full physical display. And since we do not permit ourselves the luxury of walking nude and flaunting our bodies, what is the male of the species to do? Simple. He dons a surrogate penis. And placing it around the neck is but a subterfuge. It is infinitely more subtle. And can you imagine? How inconvenient it would be to have this substitute sexual organ hanging between your legs! How quickly you would all trip!"

They had stopped staring at me. They were watching one another, wondering which one of them would stop this mad woman from continuing. I had very little left to say.

"*You*," I put a very great emphasis on this word, "dear sirs, here at Ac-Ac U. have fine-tuned the development of the surrogate penis in an academic setting. For this you are to be congratulated. The status of each of your ranks is tied to the length of the tie (read: penis). Is it a wonder then that much of the conversation one hears from the faculty wives in your part of the world revolves around the length of their husbands' ties?"

They did not seem to be in the mood to respond. One more hit should do it.

"In sum, then, gentlemen. Your tie is your public penis."

No clapping. No "that was really great, M/M." Just silence. And more silence. Schmeergang breaks it.

"This is certainly an interesting theory, M/M. An interesting theory, indeed. I am sure we all agree on that. Its validity, of course, cannot be tested. But to think that we are all deeply concerned about our sexual organs is a bit disconcerting. And then to think that our distinguished professorial ranks are deeply tied to this sexual concern is, I assure you, simply wrong. You, my dear, have come up with an interesting theory indeed. I and my other distinguished colleagues will certainly think about it. That you can be assured of. Let us for the moment get down to our work."

In Which M/M Debates with the COOCs

I was not pleased with the way Arnoldo Salvatore dismissed me. My theory was sound, I was convinced. Sure, I understood how upsetting and threatening such an idea would be to the male of the species. But he was the one involved in the act of display.

President Arnoldo Salvatore Schmeergang was continuing.

"We have a very important task before us. The Order of the Cravates, as we all know it, is at risk. How do we maintain it with all the pressures placed upon us? We are in danger of creating ambiguity. Ambiguity in the length of the ties. We must, at all cost, avoid this. Our ranks depend on the proper length of the tie. I have noticed over the years that despite the Induction Ceremony and despite my generous offer of time and help, some of our distinguished colleagues are still incapable of getting the tie at just the right length. Sometimes it is a bit below the groin. Sometimes a bit above it. How unseeming! And this is not to speak of the belly button. What a dilemma! What are we to do?"

Le Pneu raised his hand. Let us see what the golden boy would have to say.

"I agree with President Schmeergang. This is a dilemma, indeed. Quite a dilemma. What are we to do, indeed?"

That is the way, my boy, I wanted to say. Gratify the ego of your superior by repeating his words before his very eyes. He will only hear and see this. Nothing else will exist for him. This was not *imitatio dei*. This was the imitation of the father. Imitate the father and you will succeed. Dress like him. Eat like him. Look like him. Quote him amply.

All the male eyes were looking adoringly at Alphonse Le Pneu. Heads were bending in agreement. They were all speechless. After this, what was there to add?

Go for it, M/M, I told myself.

"President Schmeergang. I have an idea that may help here."

"Yes, M/M."

I read hesitation in his voice. Was he worried that I would present him with yet another theory that would leave him frightened and embarrassed?

"Well, the solution seems to me fairly clear. I noticed during the Induction Ceremony that the ties were presented to the appropriate ranks, prepared and ready to be worn. Is that right?"

"Yes. That is correct, M/M."

"Why not place a button on the tie in such a way that the mere buttoning will place the tie in the right location?"

"Hm . . . Hm . . . A button, eh? A button will, of course, mean a radical change in the structure of the tie. The addition of something new. You must understand, M/M, that we have not made a change in the tie since time immemorial. A button, eh? Where would we place it? My. My. Let us table this question and return to it after we have had our other deliberations. I might appoint a committee to look into this problem of the button. And if I do, I hope that you will agree to serve on it, M/M."

"Well, I am not . . ."

"Not now, M/M. Not now. We will discuss it later. There is another point I want you to keep in mind, my dear colleagues. As you know, we have devised the tie in such a way that its length is determined when a person is standing and not seated. Sitting obviously alters the way the tie fits. This will become important in the third topic I wish to investigate with you today. Yes, M/M?"

I had raised my hand. I had been playing with a most ridiculous idea and I wanted to see how far I could push the committee members.

"I noticed that your promotees were approximately of the same size."

I had decided not to mention Flysmudge. He was not just rotund, like his Groin colleagues. He was practically spherical.

"The length of the tie is, therefore, not a problem. But I can think of a case in my department at Pholly U. where the professor had gained so much weight that he had become approximately a ball. What provisions have you provided should this happen at Ac-Ac U.? A Professor-ès-Groin might find himself turned overnight into a Belly Button Professor. A conceivably embarrassing situation. What will you do? Put him on a diet? Have a tie made that would reach his groin but nevertheless go over his big belly?"

"Oh, my. Oh, my. You are certainly raising some thorny problems, M/M. First the button on the tie. And now the weight gain. As you were speaking, I was thinking about the exact opposite. A Belly Button Professor who loses a great deal of weight and risks endangering the higher rank. That is equally dangerous, if not downright subversive. Oh, my. Oh, my."

"President Schmeergang, if I may."

This was Le Pneu. What? Might he actually have an idea?

"It seems to me, sir, that we should think about the questions you wish to entrust us with. I am certain that I speak for everyone when I say that they must be of the utmost importance. Perhaps once we have dealt with them, we could return to the less significant matters that our distinguished guest raises."

Hah! So now I have become a distinguished guest in Le Pneu's consideration, have I? Was this progress? I was not so sure. A parrot is not a trustworthy arbiter of values.

"Well put, my boy. Well put."

Certainly, Schmeergang had no hesitation about his paternal role. Le Pneu really knew how to feed these male egos. I was fascinated by the phenomenon unfolding before me. The dialogue was carried on between Arnoldo (I liked the ring of that unorthodox name), Le Pneu, and myself. The others simply approved now of one male speaker, now of the other. Somehow I do not think that they appreciated my contributions. I had not seen a single one of them nod or smile in my direction for a while.

"Well, gentlemen. Oh, excuse me, M/M. Ha! Ha! I am so used to saying this. It comes quite naturally."

(*I am sure it does, you old sexist fart.*)

"But it is good that I slipped because that is the topic I want to investigate with you today: women at Ac-Ac U."

My ears shot up. Are we actually getting down to business?

"As you know, Ac-Ac U. is a most progressive institution."

Progressive? Five women faculty on the junior level? And I thought Pholly U. was backwards!

"We have hired five first-rate young ladies." (*Oh, God. Notice that they are not distinguished, like the males. As for young ladies, this A.S.S. was hopeless.*) "But, what are we going to do when it is time to promote them?"

I decided not to let this be a monologue on good old Arnoldo Salvatore Schmeergang's part.

"Would you mind explaining the problem to me?"

"What are we to do with the ties? What if the women are especially buxom? Could a Groin Tie then be mistaken for a Belly Button Tie?"

"Excuse me, President Schmeergang. But it seems to me that you have a potentially similar problem with a male professor, but on the opposite side of the body."

"What do you mean, M/M?"

"Males with a bowed back. That is what I mean. What do you do when professors begin to have bowed backs? A BT might conceivably then be mistaken for a GT."

"True. True. This assuredly merits the appointment of a committee. I will appoint one to study the issue. Professor Hoodwinkle, would you agree to chair this most important committee?"

P.H. started beaming. What an honor President Arnoldo Salvatore Schmeergang was bestowing on him! He would certainly love to chair this committee.

Schmeergang was continuing.

"But there is a bigger issue that has been plaguing me. Keeping me awake. Distracting me from my major duties as president of Ac-Ac U. One that relates to the promotion of women. How is it possible for us to keep the Groin Tie tradition alive? Women do not have groins. Oh, dear. Oh, dear."

I could not let this one go by.

"Excuse me, President Schmeergang. Women *do* have groins."

"What is that you say, M/M? Women and groins? How could you possibly attribute this to the fair sex?"

"Well, you know as well as I do, President Schmeergang, that were we to go by the English language, which I am certain you respect as much as I do, that we would see that the groin is a body part not distinct to the male."

"That may well be, M/M. But it is indecent. Simply indecent to associate the word 'woman' with the word 'groin'."

I decided not to let him off that easily.

"Why?"

"Why? You ask me why? Well, I will tell you. Women may have groins but the groin is not physically defined in the same way for women as it is for men. After all, women wear dresses and dresses hang loosely over that part of their body. And, hm . . . Hm . . . How are we to determine precisely where the groin is on a woman's body to be able to have the Groin Tie hang correctly? My . . . My . . . My . . . How embarrassing . . . ."

Good old Schmeergang seemed to have forgotten that I had worn nothing but pants during my days at Ac-Ac U. I could also tell from watching the committee members that not a single one of them had thought of this problem.

I knew that my next suggestion would cause an uproar.

"As a woman and as a full professor at Pholly U., might I be allowed to interject?"

"Yes, M/M."

"You see, President Schmeergang. You have stacked the cards against the entirety of the female gender. As I see it, there are two possibilities. Ac-Ac U. changes the title of the Professors-ès-Groin."

Ahhh . . . An intake of breath on everyone's part. I had committed a sacrilege. That was obvious. Was President Arnoldo Salvatore about to faint?

"My God. My God. I can't believe my ears. I simply can't believe it. Did you really suggest that we change the title? An institution that is the pride and glory of Ac-Ac U. to be changed?"

"I can't believe it either. It is simply unbelievable."

This was Parrot Le Pneu.

"O.K.," I heard myself continuing. "This suggestion is clearly out of the question. I frankly would have been surprised had you reacted any differently. Your other option, as I see it, is to disregard the cultural signification of this specific body part and simply allow the women faculty to become Professors-ès-Groin."

"Women Professors-ès-Groin?"

"Yes. Why not?"

"This is a radical departure. Do we tell our faculty to forget the meaning of this noble body part? How will the women respond to being labeled by this body part?"

"Why not ask them? After all, they are the only ones able to answer your questions. They are the ones who will be promoted with that title."

"Ask the women, huh? Do you really think, M/M, that they will be honest with us about their feelings?"

"Why should they not be? What do you have to lose by asking them? At the risk of preaching to you, gentlemen, I can assure you that the women want nothing more than to be accepted as full-fledged professionals. Let your presidency, President Arnoldo Salvatore Schmeergang, go down in the history of Ac-Ac U. as the truly progressive one. Why not be the first in the history of your distinguished institution to demystify the human body?"

I thought this plea might get to the old boy. Why not appeal to his sense of publicity and fame? I was very curious to see how he would respond.

"Would you approach the women, M/M, on our behalf?"

"Frankly, President Schmeergang, I must refuse your offer. With an adamant no. I am not a representative of the university nor do I wish to be. I am an outsider learning and observing. I have a special relationship with my women colleagues. A bond that I would not wish to jeopardize. Whether or not we speak about this issue will be our choice and what is said between us will remain confidential."

"My. My. Your words shock me, M/M."

Actually, A.S.S. did not look shocked. He looked furious. As did, I must add, all the other gentlemen in the room.

"I am surprised that you would feel so strongly after only one meeting with our women faculty. Mind you, I am trying to keep an open mind here. If you feel so strongly, so be it."

As for having the women become Professors-ès-Groin, Ac-Ac U. would have to investigate this issue as well. Schmeergang, true to form, was in the process of appointing another committee.

"Dear colleagues, I hate to burden you with yet another committee. But I assure you that this one is of great importance and significance. Women bearing our highest and oldest title."

President Arnoldo Salvatore Schmeergang was really going on about this one. I wondered who the anointed male would be. Who could possibly be entrusted with the responsibility of questioning the tradition?

"This committee chairman will, by definition, be examining and deliberating on the past, the present, and the future of our distinguished institution. Might I ask Professor Alphonse Le Pneu to bear the burden of this great task? I am sure the rest of you distinguished gentlemen will agree that no one better could represent our past, our present, and our future than this distinguished colleague. Professor Le Pneu?"

Wait a minute, I wanted to scream. Distinguished gentlemen? Have you forgotten about your very own distinguished guest? A.S.S. must have gotten so carried away with his distinguished rhetoric that he forgot all about me.

"Hmm . . . Hmm . . . Hmm . . . President Schmeergang. 'Distinguished gentlemen?'"

"Oh. M/M. I am so sorry. I forgot all about you." (*I bet you have, you old twit.*) "But I am sure you understand. This is a decision that we Ac-Ac U. old-timers alone must make. There is no possible give and take here between us and any dissenting opinions. Forgive me, my dear."

Again? I think my eyes told it all. I pointed them at him and stared so hard that he finally had to look away.

"Well, Professor Le Pneu?"

I had interrupted the flow of this august decision-making process. P.H. was fit to be tied. Since he was seated, his legs could not twitch. He more than made up for it, however, with his hands and face.

Faster than I had ever seen from him. Obviously to say he was upset would be a gross understatement.

Not to worry. We were all distracted by a movement emanating from Le Pneu's direction. His entire body moved up in the chair. Inflating. Filling up the space he was in. Was it my imagination? Or had his head become suddenly larger?

"President Schmeergang. Distinguished Colleagues."

What? A speech? Le Pneu clearly had hidden talents.

"What an honor to be asked to head this important committee! I cannot express to you how privileged I feel! A great honor, indeed, to be entrusted with this enormous task! Rest assured that the committee under my leadership will only work for the good and the glory of our distinguished institution. Any decision we make will only reflect that. Thank you for your trust in me."

President Schmeergang was beaming. His "boy" was performing according to plan. Inflating and deflating at the right moment. Never mind that it was hot air. No one noticed that.

"I can only say, Professor Le Pneu, that I am certain I speak on behalf of all of Ac-Ac U. when I express my gratitude to you for agreeing to take on this extra task. I promise you that I shall never forget it."

Congratulatory smiles were on everyone's face. We are indeed proud of ourselves, they seemed to say. We have accomplished great things.

In Which M/M Debates Again with the COOCs

Arnoldo Salvatore Schmeergang was extremely pleased with himself. He had succeeded in tabling the issue of women as Professors-ès-Groin. Since my life at Ac-Ac U. was, by necessity, to be short-lived, I was certain that this debate would not get much further than Le Pneu's committee.

"Well, distinguished colleagues. We have discussed what to do about keeping the ties the appropriate length. We have discussed what to do about women faculty. Where can we go now? I am sure that M/M will have an idea. Tell me, M/M, since Pholly U. has clearly conquered the gender problem, what burning issues are they debating now?"

"If I may, President Schmeergang, correct you on your last point . . ."

Were the assembled faces about to fall off? Or did they simply look like it? I had learned that one can take many liberties as a visitor in an institution, having watched male colleagues do it over the years. Let these fools live and learn.

"Yes?"

"You see, to say that Pholly U. has conquered the gender problem is a gross exaggeration. Pholly U. is as far from this as one can be. I will be happy to share some statistics with you. Statistics on salaries. Statistics on hirings. Statistics on promotions. And then you can perhaps tell me whether you still feel that Pholly U. is the progressive institution that you think it is. Let me assure you, gentlemen, that I am the exception and not the rule for that august institution."

"Sure. Sure. Whatever you wish . . ."

I could tell that Schmeergang merely said this to dismiss me. He had already convinced himself of one thing: women were at the top of the world at Pholly U. After all, was I not living proof of that?

"But I am not here to explain to you the weaknesses of Pholly U. Gender, gentlemen, is not the only burning issue. You must now think about promoting the handicapped."

As I said this, I was carefully watching Professor Assam. Would he speak up now or would he simply sit back as he has been doing during this entire meeting?

"The handicapped? What do you mean? We have always hired the handicapped."

"In all my weeks here, I have not seen a single visually handicapped individual. Nor have I seen anyone in a wheelchair. On the faculty, that is."

"Oh, my. Oh, my. That is true, M/M, isn't it? But, you know, my dear . . ."

Was Arnoldo Salvatore trying to put me off again? Well, I promised myself, it will not work.

"You know, this is a complicated matter."

"Aren't they all, President Schmeergang?"

He acted as if he did not hear me.

"Bear with me for a moment, M/M. Let us assume for a moment that we do promote a blind individual to tenure at our distinguished university. How can we be sure that when he ties his tie, it will be in the right position? If he is merely a Belly Button Professor, and misses the length, he might confuse people into thinking that he is a Professor-ès-Groin. Or if he is of our highest rank, how can we assure that he will always hit the right spot? Can you imagine the havoc that this would create in our midst?"

"Mind you, I do not agree with your position. Let me, for the moment, follow in your logic, President Schmeergang, and assume that it may not be in your best interest to hire the visually handicapped. However, they are not the only disabled, you know."

"Right you are, M/M. I myself have nothing against those people, you understand. But let us imagine we hire someone in a wheelchair. There are plenty of those running around. Ha! Ha!"

President Schmeergang was chuckling at his own joke. No sooner had he completed his second "ha," than the rest of his male compatriots smiled. How wonderful to be a university president with all your underlings reinforcing your every move!

"Sure, this man will be able to tie his tie. But, my God, what is to happen when he sits down. How will people know the length of his tie? Do we ask him to stand in the wheelchair when he appears in public? What if he cannot stand? I can only see more and more confusion. Dear me! Dear me! I am afraid I will have to put my foot down on this one. Hiring women will just have to do for now. I repeat: I myself have nothing against the handicapped. But I really do not believe they would be happy at Ac-Ac U."

Why did this argument sound so familiar? Was it because I had heard it over and over on search committees at Pholly U.? What altruism, someone overhearing these comments might wish to say! No!! This is not concern over a candidate's happiness. This dismissal is the last recourse of the bigoted. I had learned something during my years in academia. When certain justifications surface, the discussion is over. The argument over happiness was one such.

I think that Arnoldo Salvatore Schmeergang was actually surprised by my silence. I had, after all, been countering him repeatedly during the meeting of the COOCs. Everyone else was watching me. I said nothing and waited for the next step.

"My dear colleagues. This has been a most enlightening gathering. I want to thank you all for your incisive comments."

With this, our noble president got up, signaling us that the official meeting was over. I was still trying to figure out what these comments were to which Schmeergang was referring when I was accosted by P.H. His twitching had stopped.

"M/M. You certainly . . ."

I realized too late that I had tuned P.H. out. His words of wisdom are lost forever. I had merely smiled for the entirety of his little speech. I was, to be honest, more interested in the activities of Alphonse Le Pneu. He was clearly the hit of the afternoon. Arnoldo Salvatore Schmeergang had already put his arm around him in a gesture of friendship and affection. The two, surrounded by the other committee members, were being escorted out of the room.

In Which M/M Reads the DULL Newsletter

The meeting with the COOCs had really worn me out. S. P.-T. was a good listener. She purred and presented me with her belly to stroke.

"I am finding these committees too strenuous, my little one. I am not sure that I can attend any more of their meetings."

I had decided to spend the evening at home writing in my diary and just digesting all that I had encountered so far at Ac-Ac U. Time was moving quickly. My briefcase was overflowing with mail that I had collected from my DULL mailbox. Notices upon notices. Most migrated directly from my briefcase to the Guest House garbage can. A distinguished trajectory.

Drawing my attention was a set of chartreuse sheets, folded over and stapled. I pulled them out from the collection of otherwise nondescript announcements. And there in all its glory was the DULL Newsletter. I love newsletters. I always have. I announced to S. P.-T. that she and I were in for a pleasurable moment indeed. She jumped up on the couch and the two of us proceeded to feast our eyes on this masterpiece.

Pictures mixed with prose to entertain the DULL reader. But I discovered that this joy was not restricted to my cherished department: copies of the newsletter were circulated around the campus. No one could escape the chartreuse sheets. A brief history of the department graced the first page. Professor Hirsute-du-Vigneron and Professor Assam, standing and smiling at one another, were immortalized in a pose in the chair's office. "Outgoing Chairman Hands the Mantle of Leadership to the New Chairman," read the headline. S. P.-T. and I decided to forego that article.

I skimmed the rest of the rag to see if there was anything else of interest. And lo and behold, in the middle of the newsletter, was a surprise item. One brought to us by popular request. It seems that the departmental readership was curious about a particularly savory dish that made an appearance at every annual departmental picnic. "Trust us," the article said, "if awards were given for the dish of the decade, it would go to this." "This" was Professor Kupferhoff's "Hungarian Goulash." For the more enterprising academic, Professor Kupferhoff had kindly agreed to provide the recipe for this popular item.

"We are not here just to give you intellectual sustenance," the editors argued. "We want to have healthy and well-fed friends and colleagues. The physical repast is just as important as the intellectual one."

I was more and more intrigued by these "editors." Who were they? Why were they always addressing their readership in the plural "we?" An even bigger surprise awaited me: Hirsute-du-Vigneron and Assam were the proud fathers of this publication. I turned to S. P.-T. and confessed to her that I would not be amazed if this showed up as a publication on their respective annual reports! I could swear that she laughed.

An interview with the chair. A recipe for the DULL dish of the decade. What was to be next? Incredible: The announcement of a new course! This took me by surprise. The semester was well on its way and a new course was in the newsletter? Hirsute-du-Vigneron and Assam had devoted an entire page to this latest DULL brainchild. I wondered if this was to be the course of my dreams? No. Fortunately, this beauty was not offered this academic year. "How to Speak to Aliens." Aliens did not mean the holders of a green card but those "little critters that populate the other parts of the galaxy." Thus did Professor Humbert Linguano describe his mission.

It was not normal DULL procedure to announce its courses in its newsletter but it was very proud of this particular course and was publicizing it as an attempt to help launch Professor Linguano's new book: *Alienese*. I looked into the smiling face of Professor Linguano whose shining bald head was offset by a hefty beard. Thick glasses completed the outfit. The departmental camera had caught him standing stiffly, cradling the open book in his arms. How touching, I thought! Hirsute-du-Vigneron and Assam had not neglected to provide the readership with the complete bibliographic citation for this wondrous work: Ac-Ac: DULL Publications, Mimeographed Series, #909.

My curiosity got the better of me. In a minute, I had P.H. on the phone. He had, after all, always insisted on his willingness to answer any questions for me. Up till now, I had refrained from calling him at home. The DULL publication series? Oh, yes. He knew all about that. Of course, he was more than willing to satiate me with information about this distinguished series.

Good, I said to myself. The code word. It bodes well.

"You see, M/M. I helped found the series. It is a great honor that redounds upon DULL. Only a professor in the department itself may publish in it. Why do you ask? Would you like us to consider one of your own publications for the series? You are, after all, a member of DULL."

"Oh. No. Heavens, no. I had been reading the DULL Newsletter and . . ."

P.H. was quick to interrupt me. Had I insulted him by my quick refusal of his offer?

"Ah. Yes. Our latest publication. *Alienese*. A work in which Professor Humbert Linguano outlines his theories (for they are numerous) on that language. He discusses its grammatical properties, its sound patterns, and so on. It is a wonderful work. Groundbreaking. This is, of course, private information but I feel I can share it with you. The committee was overwhelmed with Professor Linguano's charts. What a linguist. We were unanimous in our endorsement of his manuscript."

"Why #909?"

"An important question, M/M. An important question. #909 testifies to the activity of our distinguished DULL faculty. Nine hundred and eight works have preceded it. Some, I am certain, would interest you. Fine masterpieces of literary scholarship."

"Really?"

"Oh, yes. The best plot summaries to be found anywhere. Some of our young scholars have dedicated themselves to this enterprise. I will let you in on a secret, M/M. These summaries are better than reading the original. Yes, if I do say so myself. They are wonderful. Absolutely wonderful."

I decided to bring P.H. back to earth. Why not ask him about the distribution for this series of which he was so fond. True, these works are mimeographed, P.H. was quick to explain to me. But this should by no means keep me from realizing how important the series is. The DULL faculty was most serious. Not like those prima donnas in some other departments who only pursue fame and fortune. Besides, what is important after all? Mimeographing these works makes them cheaper and allows direct distribution to students.

"But, don't you think, Professor Hoodwinkle, that there might be a conflict of interest somewhere here?"

"What? A conflict of interest? Let us not be ridiculous. Please. Our faculty is only concerned with one thing: the greater glory of knowledge. We have always sold our works directly to the students. DULL is to be complimented on the fact that its series is so widely available."

P.H.'s free advertisement was far from effective. S. P.-T. and I thanked our lucky stars that we did not need his mimeographed series to publish our work.

The evening's entertainment was far from over. P.H.'s last words had lulled me into leafing through the newsletter over and over again. And there on the last page was a column: "DULL Proudly Presents: FUTURE DULLARDS!" I read on. "Dear Reader," it began. "Our happiness overflows. Our pride is endless. We are not always able to present you with this column." I could see Hirsute-du-Vigneron and Assam beaming. The occasion for the column? The birth of two male children to two different DULL professors. And since pregnancies did not come to fruition on the occasion of every newsletter, this was a special treat.

"Imagine, S. P.-T. What would we have done had we landed here at a time of no births?"

The celebration of childbearing had been a long tradition that dated from the founding of DULL. The DULL family was not just an intellectual unit. The babies were there smiling at the reader of the DULL newsletter. Brief biographies of the two males graced the photographs. Their names, weight, and height were to be forever imprinted on the historical memory of DULL. What a future there was for this distinguished department! Would that I could have been here for the birth of a girl! Would Hirsute-du-Vigneron and Assam have been so eloquent and so emotional?

I had never been a big one on families. But moving them into the workplace was more than I could tolerate. I was beginning to wonder how long I could stomach being in this department.

In Which M/M Has Second Thoughts about Her Visiting Appointment

P.H. spotted me in the morning wandering the DULL hallway. Reading newsletters and memos was the opposite of intellectual stimulation. I had only gone up in the hot air balloon, after all, to take a break from Pholly U. I had not packed any reading material. What a dilemma! S. P.-T. was also beginning to show signs of distress. The term was only half over and there I was already thinking about its end. What was there for me to look forward to in my singular learning experience?

"You look distressed, M/M."

"As a matter of fact, Professor Hoodwinkle, I am thinking about my return to Pholly U. I think that my colleagues would not want me to extend my absence for more than a semester."

Was I kidding? My colleagues could not stand my guts. Needless to say, the feeling was quite mutual. So why not stay away for a longer period? Maybe a hell one knows is better than one one does not know.

"What are you trying to say, M/M?"

"I think, Professor Hoodwinkle, that I will return to my own institution when this semester comes to an end at Ac-Ac U."

"Are you sure you don't want to reconsider, M/M? There is so much we need to learn from you. But you know best. You know that we will miss you."

Learn from me? My experience with the COOCs had convinced me that these Ac-Ac U. officials had shut down their brains. There was no space for new information. Their hard disks had not yet crashed but their floppy disks were permanently in the write protection mode. Nothing could penetrate. Still, I was torn. I wanted to see the women faculty once more. I had also been promised glimpses into some of the more secret committees at Ac-Ac U.

P.H. confessed that he had stopped me, not so much because he was concerned about my emotional state, but because he had a surprise for his visitor. A surprise?

In Which M/M Attends the
Muted Language Society Award Ceremony

Yes, a surprise. And what a surprise this was! A private invitation to the most prestigious award ceremony at Ac-Ac U. Very private. Very hush-hush. P.H. could not even reveal to me anything other than the name of the society presenting this award: the Muted Language Society. By tradition, the identity of the lucky candidate had always remained a secret until the night of the ceremony. Only the inner committee of the society was privy to his name. Should I have been shocked? P.H. was on the committee. My landing on Ac-Ac was timed perfectly. My patron could not have been chosen better.

My luck was not about to run out. Nor was my entertainment. P.H. was my official escort to this exclusive event. And there we were, once again, in the president's mansion. Was it the same place in which the Induction into the Order of the Cravates had taken place? I think so. But the completely different floor arrangement made it difficult to see this immediately. The room decoration was infinitely classier. Nothing like the seating at that earlier event. Less chairs. More fancy furniture. Flower arrangements standing proudly on side tables. And parading around the room were tuxedo-garbed gentlemen carrying trays of champagne and delicacies.

Need I even mention that I was the only woman in the room? By now, many of the faces looked familiar to me. Missing was President Arnoldo Salvatore Schmeergang himself. Was he going to make a grand appearance like he did for the Induction Ceremony?

Music was being piped in. Soft and non-intrusive. So much so that it took a few minutes to realize that we were all being serenaded. And then: boom. Drums replaced the soft music. And behold, the door opened and in walked President Schmeergang with a Groin Tie, whom I took to be the happy winner of this coveted award. They were arm in arm. Both dressed in dark suits. Schmeergang's characteristic bow tie was shining. Was it silk, I wondered, or some kind of phosphorescent material? He looked rather silly, partly because his face was plastered with the biggest shit-eating grin I have ever beheld. As for the Groin Tie? His extremely thick glasses made his eyes look enormous. He looked petrified. If he were not walking attached to Arnoldo, I think he would have taken a quick tumble to the floor. At the same time, he looked familiar. Where had I seen that face?

The drum roll was replaced by President Schmeergang's booming voice.

"Dear friends."

Oh. No colleagues here? So now we were all friends? Was this a sign of the dignity and exclusive nature of the happening?

"Dear friends. Dear friends. I am overwhelmed with emotion. We are all gathered here at a special occasion: the presentation of the Muted Language Society Award. Need I emphasize the importance of this award? Need I stress its intimate and long history with our distinguished institution? How proud I am to be standing in this room presenting the award to this lucky winner! How well I remember when I myself was its recipient! Ah! To share in the glory of this moment. This, my dear friends, is what makes Ac-Ac U. the special and distinguished institution it is."

There was a twinkle in old Arnoldo's eyes. Was he about to burst into tears? Maybe I should be a bit more overwhelmed myself.

"Yes. Dear friends. I and the winner of this award, as is traditional, have walked arm in arm before your eyes. The award joins us physically as it does intellectually. You are all here to share in this celebration. In this glory. Friends, may I present to you the winner of this year's Muted Language Society Award, Professor J. P. Snootpile, Professor-ès-Groin, author of *Texts Utter, People Stutter.*"

So. That is who he is. Now I knew why that face looked so familiar. I had spotted him at the DULL reception, but had not gotten the chance to meet him. I had read about Snootpile's fame in the DULL Newsletter. There under the faculty listing of activities, he had the longest entry.

"Professor Snootpile is a shining light at Ac-Ac U."

Schmeergang was outdoing himself. But I sensed that nothing could stop him.

"His reputation is deservedly international. He has trained a record number of students who now populate universities all over the world. Over the years, I have watched Ac-Ac U. increase in distinction and, in no small measure, this is due to Professor Snootpile's activities. How fortunate for us that we have been able to increase colleagues' contact with my dear friend, J. P. Snootpile, by placing his appointment in two different administrative units. He enriches, on the one hand, a department that is already distinguished in its own right, the Department of Unusual Languages and Literatures. On the other hand, Professor Snootpile has been instrumental in reviving the Program of Universal Studies. I am aware that some of you have heard this program affectionately referred to as PUS. But, as most of you also know, I am very much against acronyms. They largely demean and belittle our fine and distinguished departments."

I had noticed that President Schmeergang was quite careful not to use my own department's initials. No words like DULL should probably be uttered on this "distinguished" occasion.

"But I digress. Dear friends. I can only say that the award committee could not have chosen a worthier candidate for this year's Muted Language Society Award than Professor Snootpile and his *Texts Utter, People Stutter*. Need I remind you that the award is earmarked for the book that is most likely to maintain our values? I have been privileged to read this work and I hope you will allow me to quote from the words of the jury:

> At a time when new critical schools are threatening to rip the fabric of our intellectual world—if not of our society—it is refreshing to see a book like that of Professor Snootpile. The book contains ample quotations. 99% (yes, that is correct, ninety-nine percent) of his book is formed of quotations. This allows the reader to bask in the glory of the texts that comprise the largest part of our great civilization. Snootpile's absent prose is a credit to the profession. Ac-Ac University is to be congratulated for encouraging this high level of scholarly endeavor.

"How fondly, over all these years, has Professor Snootpile insisted to me that we must let the texts speak for themselves. So much so, dear friends, that I would slap him on the back whenever we met and say: 'Hello, Snootpile. How is I'll-let-the-text-speak-for-itself today?'"

There was some giggling around the room.

"Mind you, I have asked my long-time friend, Professor Snootpile, if I could reveal this most intimate detail to you and he was in agreement. A great intellectual with a generous soul! A rare combination indeed! And what a model of scholarship! 'Absent prose!' I could not have expressed it better. Professor Snootpile, you are the model we should all imitate. Faculty and graduate students alike must be

encouraged to walk in your footsteps. Dear friends, join me in congratulating the proud winner of this year's Muted Language Society
Award, Professor 'Absent Prose' Snootpile."

Clapping filled the room. All were overcome with emotion. It
was time to shake Snootpile's hand. A line was forming and P.H. and
I simply joined it.

"Heartiest Congratulations."

"Thank you."

"Heartiest Congratulations."

"Thank you."

These words, repeated over and over again, were the only ones I
could hear. When it was my turn to approach Ac-Ac U.'s shining light,
I mouthed the same words. And what a vision this shining light was!
I had been too far away during Schmeergang's speech to notice much
about Snootpile. There he was. His dark suit was peppered with little
white droppings, which I took to be dandruff. His Groin Tie had eaten
lunch at the same time he had. Most likely it had been fed a generous
helping of mayonnaise from an overly full sandwich. And what a
breath on that old fossil! He reeked of old wine and rotten onions. This
was obviously the greatest moment of his career. I noticed his left hand
kept rising to his eyes, in what I first interpreted as a nervous gesture.
But no. He was trying to clear away the tears. Touching.

"Absent prose," huh? I sensed that Snootpile and his scholarly
ideals would fit right into Pholly U. without a problem. Creativity was
not the most easily found commodity at my dearly beloved home university.

In Which M/M Meets the Women Faculty Once Again

Why was it that these ceremonies were driving me slowly mad? I told S. P.-T. who, by this time, was beginning to show signs of disgust. Ac-Ac U. was obviously driving her crazy as well. I confessed to her that we would not spend much longer in this strange place.

On one of my walks across the Ac-Ac U. campus to some meeting or other, I had run across B. We hugged one another like long lost friends. Why not have another wine and cheese party, I suggested? At my place?

Once again, the group of women faculty was there. And once again, S. P.-T. sat looking at us. Obviously pleased that I had other friends with whom I could share some of my more ridiculous experiences. It was good to have the wine flowing again. I was not sure how much of the private meetings I could reveal to my friends.

Fortunately, A piped up. She wanted to share a story with us. She had just uncovered the saga of Professor Giovanni Kleinputz. A Groin Tie in the Department of Ecstasy. Listening to her answer questions from her younger colleagues made me realize that the Department of Ecstasy was what was known in the rest of the world as the Department of Religion. Professor Kleinputz had been the chair of the department.

"Imagine. Imagine if you can."

Our storyteller was beginning.

"Imagine a St. Francis-like figure. With clerical tonsure. St. Francis had the hole in his hair by choice. Professor Kleinputz had it there by heredity. Poor fellow. As much as St. Francis loved the birds, so Professor Kleinputz loved the bottle. Forgive me, St. Francis."

A had her hands together in prayer and her eyes directed skywards as she begged the saint's indulgence.

I was already laughing. So were my friends. I would swear that even S. P.-T. was grinning.

"But the bottle would be Kleinputz's downfall. He drank and drank and drank some more. Then once upon a time, in Kleinputz's short-lived administrative life, there came a search. As chair of the department, his was the job of entertaining the visiting candidate. When the candidate did not appear at his next appointment, Kleinputz's phone rang. It rang and rang and rang some more. No answer. The Associate Chair of Ecstasy suspected the worst. He rushed to Kleinputz's house. And there, sprawled on the floor, in a drunken stupor, was Kleinputz with his arm around the sleeping male candidate. The Associate Chair was in a tizzy. What was to be done? What if the candidate squealed? True, he was drunk. But what would he remember upon waking? The solution came to him in a flash. Offer the position to this lucky young man. Fortunately, the seduced gentleman had another, more prestigious offer so Kleinputz was safe once more."

We, A's listeners, were on the edges of our chairs. Unsure whether to be overcome by laughter or disgust. There was more to come. A was continuing.

"As he drank and drank some more, Kleinputz was deteriorating. His choice of alcohol had become more refined. Now he only indulged in vodka. To make things worse, he developed a taste for candy bars. They could only be eaten and then washed down with the vodka. You might all want to ask: How did he function? You will be surprised to learn that he functioned very well. The students suspected that their professor was not quite all there. But if some of them had ended up in Flysmudge's class, would this have been any different?"

I was fascinated. But perhaps not overly shocked.

"What did Professor Kleinputz teach?"

"You see, M/M, his specialty gave him some maneuvering room. For years, he had taught 'Introduction to Meditation.' A bit of this. A bit of that. And a lot of meditation. If you passed by his lecture room—which for the record was always overpacked—you would be met by silence. If you were courageous and looked in, your eyes would have feasted on throngs of students sitting still, eyes closed. Were they thinking higher thoughts about their spiritual experience? Or were they thinking about their dates on Saturday nights? We will never know."

"Why does this make me think of that DULL course I heard about, 'Sleeping through the Ages?'" This was from C.

"You are absolutely right, C. The similarities are enormous. Both really attract students and have enormous waiting lists. Both are held in the same auditorium. Both, by a happy coincidence, are held back to back so that the same students can benefit from the two star teachers. What a great way to add to your beauty sleep!

"Kleinputz's saga had a very happy ending. The administration had never heard of the incident with the male candidate. His department was ecstatic (excuse the pun) about his student numbers. So they nominated him for an endowed chair. The Serene Wrap Chair in Ecstasy.

"Sure Kleinputz was a drunkard. But he knew the value and worth of being a chair. To say that he had thought about it in his sober moments would be an understatement. He would admit that to anyone who cared to listen. But the Serene Wrap Chair? That was more than any one could dream of. For years his wife had been wrapping his sandwiches in it. No disrespect intended BUT did they not for years use Grapple Bags in the house for everything from kitchen garbage to children's diapers?

"A reception was held in honor of Professor Kleinputz. Tears welled in his eyes as he declared to all present that his joy was beyond compare: 'Thank you all. Thank you all. I am speechless.'

"That was, from what I hear," A was continuing, "the extent of Kleinputz's speech at the reception held in his honor by the president's office. Some of his savvier colleagues wondered if he was quite all there. But since he was able to stand during the entire ordeal, no one was any the wiser."

"You know, A, I have trouble believing the stories you are telling me."

"Why do you say that, M/M? Doesn't Pholly U. have some nuts of its own?"

"A very good point. I am sure that the place is full of them. I, frankly, however, usually try to steer clear of my colleagues and their adventures. When gossip reaches me, it is never this juicy."

In Which M/M Has a Nightmarish Experience

As we women clinked our glasses, I found myself transported, as in a dream, to the award ceremony for Professor Kleinputz. There I was standing with the best and the proudest of the male Ac-Ac U. faculty. There I was joining in all the merriment. Thoughts flooded my head as Kleinputz delivered his words of non-wisdom. What if I should ever receive the Liquid Bummer Chair? Or the Softer-than-Life Toilet Tissue Chair? I was hallucinating. A voice awoke me:

"Wasn't that a simply heart-warming speech?" It was P.H. The jerk was always there. He was really beginning to get on my nerves.

"You know, M/M. It has only been topped by the Rotor Tooter Chair."

I was speechless. Worse, I was beginning to realize that even my own worst imaginings could never keep up with the reality of Ac-Ac U.

Kleinputz's party seemed to be going on forever. How was I going to exit it gracefully? Clink.

In Which M/M Is Back in the Guest House

Clink. Clink.

"M/M, are you okay?" D was bending over me. Full of concern.

"Yes. I am fine. I seem to have blacked out for a moment."

How fortunate that the clink brought me back to the land of the living. This was surely a sign. The male establishment of Ac-Ac U. was managing to invade my mind at times when I was supposed to be free of it. A bad, bad sign. More than ever, I was convinced that it was time for me to leave this academically isolated haven for intellectually misshapen males.

But, for now, back to the party. I was afraid that any more stories from A would cause my mind to be invaded once more. These males were certainly insistent. Escaping them was proving more and more difficult. The solution?

I had remembered from our last meeting that B was the one who was most interested in my poetry. Had she herself written any? I decided to take the plunge.

"B. I would love to hear some of your poetry."

"What? How did you know I wrote poetry?"

"Just a lucky guess."

"Well, M/M, I am as reluctant to recite my poetry as you are. I should add that I am not a published poet so the poems simply emanate from me on odd occasions."

"I understand. But please humor me just this once."

"Only if you promise me one thing. That we will have one of your poems for every one of mine."

B was driving a hard bargain. I felt emotionally drained from my unexpected appearance of sorts at Kleinputz's reception.

"Why not?" I heard my own voice answering. I must admit that I shocked myself.

"But with the same limitations as before. No comments after the poems."

I had not revealed to the women faculty at Ac-Ac U. that my days at their august institution were numbered. I hated good-byes. I hated them more than anything else in the world. They were probably more distasteful to me than even the male windbags with whom I came in contact on a daily basis at Pholly U. I would have to leave the women faculty at Ac-Ac U. to their own wiles. I was hoping that they would keep up these get-togethers, if only to draw strength from one another.

B was beginning. Her voice was shaking a bit. I tried to look encouraging.

> bald.
> forehead shining.
> nose protruding.
> the He in power enters the room.
> try as i might.
> i can never be bald.
> my forehead may shine.
> my nose may protrude.
> i will remain a She.

B looked embarrassed. I decided to plunge into one of my own poems. An action designed to distract her.

> I ask for a key
> The fiend responds
> A cardinal sin
> Have I done
> The treasures inside
> Are not to be had.
> Should I have said:
> Open Sesame?
> Should I have rubbed
> Aladdin's lamp?
>
> No.
> The *Arabian Nights* are fantasy.
> No rubies are behind that door.
> No diamonds are behind that door.
> Doors cannot be opened . . .
> Treasures cannot be had . . .
> By a woman

I could see B's eyes lighting up. She wanted to ask me questions. Just like last time. No. I was going to resist this. I never discuss my writings. But I felt that my poem was functioning like an answer to hers. We were moving in the same universe. That would hopefully encourage her to continue her writing.

E was clearing her throat. She was not a poet. But that is all right. I feel she needs to be encouraged. She has said hardly anything at our get-togethers. She is always aloof. Sitting outside the group. And her clothing! Her unbelievable clothing! I so much wanted to ask her why she dressed in this fashion but did not want to invade her privacy. Was this clearing of the throat a beginning?

"You know, M/M. Your poem about verbal battering . . ."

"Yes, E?"

"I have been thinking about it. Ever since our last meeting. I am not quite sure how to begin."

She was hesitant. But there was an urgency in her voice.

"Why not at the beginning?"

"You have probably noticed my outfits."

How could I miss them, I wanted to respond. But I did not. I did not want her to feel that I was silencing her. I looked at her with as much attention as I could muster. I felt that this might be a matter of professional life and death for her.

"I did not dress like this on my arrival at Ac-Ac U. My appearance was more relaxed, more informal. Until one day that I will never never forget."

I was not the only one sitting on the edge of my chair. Every one else was in the same position. I was sure that E had never spoken to anyone about this special day.

"The senior Groin Tie in my department called me in and told me that I did not dress right. According to him, all the Professors-ès-Groin and all the Belly Button Professors in the department had come to the same conclusion. That if I did not change my clothing, my chances for moving up were sharply reduced. I went out that same day and changed my entire wardrobe."

I wanted to say that I could not believe it. But who the hell would I be kidding? She was clearly looking for a response from me. Who the hell was I to give her advice?

"You know, E. I believe that if you were to probe any of us, you would find horrific stories. That if we were to paint our professional lives, the paintings would not be too dissimilar. The colors might vary. The shapes might vary. But I am firmly convinced that the substance would be the same.

"May I be self-indulgent and tell you a story about my thesis advisor, Thornwipple?"

The name alone brought a smile to E's face. A good start. The others were suppressing a smile. They were unsure whether to laugh or cry.

"I am afraid I will have to ask A's indulgence. I am not the storyteller she is. Good old Thornwipple. He never was big on ideas. But was he so lacking in them that he needed to steal my ideas and peddle them off as his own at conferences? I, like you, will never forget that. My first paper at a professional meeting. The female graduate student. The male big wigs. Those whose books and articles I had already chewed thoroughly. They invited me to the bar after my paper to share a few drinks with them. I was awed. Let us admit it. But my awe turned into shock as I heard that old geezer spitting out my ideas. All the bald heads listened intently and respectfully, agreeing with these bold new ideas. Ah, yes, that was my first initiation into the world of truth and learning. Over the years, I would come to learn from female friends and colleagues whose tongues were lubricated with a few scotches that my experience was not unusual."

Was this a comfort to E? To know that she was not alone? Yet what kind of comfort would this be to know that she was destined to these pleasures by her gender?

"You know, E, for a while I polished my nails. When I was a budding young professor. But the bright and expensive nail polish could not hide the dirt and bruises that were embedded in my finger nails from clawing my way up in the system."

E looked quite upset. I sensed that she was torn between my advice and that of the senior male Groin Ties in her department. I was not sure whether I should entertain her with any more of my stories. After all, her academic future was bound to be different from my academic past. I was fortunate not to be at Ac-Ac U.

Silence. It was also fortunate that D had an early morning appointment. The gathering had to come to an end. Once more, there were hugs all around. This time, I did not say that we should do it again. I would most likely have disappeared from the world of Ac-Ac U. by the next meeting of the women faculty. The ways of academe are indeed mysterious. My new-found female friends at Ac-Ac U. would have to find their own way.

In Which M/M Muses about Her Social Life as a Woman at Ac-Ac U.

These evenings spent with the women faculty were like a breath of fresh air for me. It took me a while to realize why. My days were always filled with activity and my nights were dedicated to writing. My life at Ac-Ac U. had revolved around the males. Sure, there had been plenty of dinner parties. But they had been restricted to restaurants. Sure, I was a celebrity. But the Groin Ties were afraid to introduce me to their wives. Deep down inside they did not think me normal. Would I seduce their wives? That was the big question. The seduction, of course, did not even have to be physical. My mere presence represented a danger zone. I was the other possibility lurking behind the horizon. A different life choice for all these women. Had I been at Ac-Ac U. instead of Pholly U., it might mean that I could be a Groin Tie by now. What confusion for that distinguished male establishment! What wonderful chaos I could have created!

P.H. had explained to me quite proudly that the wives of the Ac-Ac U. professors were very supportive "good little girls" (read: unlike you, M/M). They made their hubbies' lunch. And what grateful hubbies they were! One could see them munching the sandwiches, savoring every bite in the appropriate university locations. Departmental seminar rooms became dens of crunching mouths at lunch time. It had taken me a while to figure out that when individuals "did lunch" at Ac-Ac U., it meant that each took out his respective sandwich and gobbled it in the company of the other. Each priding himself on the fact that his sandwich was thicker. I wondered: what was the relationship between the thick sandwich and the length of the tie? Were wives here sublimating their own desires and ambitions into thick sandwiches? I would never discover the answer to this question. The wives were not to come into contact with the visitor from outer space.

Not only was lunch lovingly prepared, but wifey had dinner on the table when hubby arrived home. (All this I had learned from P.H. during one of his ramblings.) She might even entertain his students when he needed it.

"Aren't wives wonderful, M/M?" This had been P.H.'s conclusion.

I decided to reply to that.

"I really wouldn't know, Professor Hoodwinkle. But aren't mores changing? What about same-sex couples?"

"God forbid, M/M. Homosexual couples? This is an aberration of nature. Can you imagine? Oh, my! Oh, my! Oh, my!"

I would swear that from that moment on Hoodwinkle looked at me with suspicion. Was I possibly a lesbian? You old fart. You can keep guessing. I so much wanted to tell him about the time I came into the department office at Pholly U. sporting an especially short haircut. My pot-bellied hee-hawing chair*man* let out a big laugh and asked me if I had become a lesbian. A classic.

Ac-Ac U. Pholly U. The two were beginning to be quasi-synonymous for me. Did that mean it was time to leave? Oh, come on, M/M, I told myself. Do not be so quick to give up. Surely, Ac-Ac U. can still teach you something.

In Which M/M Finally Attends the Promotion Committee Meeting

Sure enough. Here it was at last. The Promotion Committee Meeting. In which certain members of the lowly ranks of Ac-Ac U. find themselves facing either eternal damnation or eternal salvation. I had had a bit of experience with promotions at Pholly U., but I was sure that this would be an experience all its own. After all, had not everything else proved unique at Ac-Ac U.?

Dean Gloopersnort had been gracious enough to send me a personal invitation to this committee. The usual verbiage. What an important committee it was. How important my function would be on it. And on and on and on. He was not giving me a choice. Nor did I want one. After all, how could I forego one of the pleasures of Ac-Ac U.?

I walked into Gloopersnort's special seminar room. The repository of the promotion files. Stacks of dossiers overflowed onto the tables. Color-coded. From No Tie to Belly Button Tie. From Belly Button Tie to Groin Tie. There they were. The pride and glory of Ac-Ac U. I wondered what secrets these dossiers embodied. Teaching evaluations and publications. Supporting letters. Marvelous examples of lives dedicated to the pursuit of knowledge. Or so one would think.

I had been spending a bit of time reading the dossiers in Gloopersnort's office. By decanal order, the materials could not circulate. Should I have been surprised that no one was ever with me during those hours of reading? It was as if the materials would be better judged unread.

During one of those seemingly endless hours of sitting alone with Ac-Acian promotion rhetoric, I was somehow transported to Pholly U. One unforgettable promotion dossier. One which had left me quite stunned at the time. Never in my academic existence had I seen such a dossier. Its sheer mass was astounding. As one walked into the Pholly U. Dean's Office, one was assaulted by this dossier. It towered over the others. This was clearly someone who had no shame about his intellectual size. Reams and reams of black notebooks lay on top of one another. Numbered in series. This wonder of academia back in my home university had carefully cut up his publications into bite-sized pieces of about three inches by five inches and glued these pieces onto larger sheets of paper. The sheets had then been gathered together, giving birth in the process to reams and reams of sheets, all sequentially numbered and then arranged into black notebooks. These had been numbered in turn. Each of them held approximately two hundred pages and there were ten of them. Uniformity in publication was the argument for this grandiose gesture. Inflation was how I interpreted it.

Was I the only one then who had been annoyed by this procedure? It seemed like it at the time. The members of the Pholly U. promotion committee had hovered over the dossier, like vultures over carrion. Was it dead meat or intellectual sustenance they were after? The answer does not matter now. They could barely keep their hands off the materials. As if they were trying to inhale the essence of the weighty tomes through their fingers.

"A genius!"

"Oh. Yes. A marvel!"

"My. My. The best dossier it has been my privilege to read over my entire career at Pholly U."

And on and on and on. Our insecure male (for I had naively believed that this inflation was but a sign of his insecurity) had assured himself a future that would be the envy of all his Pholly male colleagues for many years to come.

Just thinking about this successful trick made my blood boil—even years after the event and even here at Ac-Ac U.

I told myself to calm down. Maybe things would be different at Ac-Ac U. After all, the discussions had not yet taken place nor had the votes been tallied.

Time for the meeting. I spotted P.H. entering the room. He threw a smile my way. We all sat around the table. Need I mention that I was the only woman there? Or is that superfluous by now? (I suspect the latter!) Some of the faces were familiar to me. Others were not. Surprise of surprises. There was no one from DULL. Did that bode well or ill? Gloopersnort had not explained the system of selection to me nor did I really want to know. I was sure it would involve some "distinguished" colleagues. So, why bother?

By the way the committee members were chatting, it became obvious that this was to be a more informal meeting than the previous official functions I had attended. People were actually speaking without having to wait for the appropriate authority figure to give them the signal to do so.

Dean Gloopersnort walked in. Smiling. His Groin Tie tied and hanging beautifully. I was sure wifey had approved his appearance before he walked out of the house this morning. He took his place at the head of the table. The natural locus of power.

I sensed that this was a committee whose members had worked together before. They were relaxed and looked at one another with knowing glances. Would the procedure be explained to me? Sure enough. It was as if Gloopersnort had read my mind.

"Welcome, friends."

As far as I was concerned, that said it all. The intimacy of the situation was assured.

"We are here today to decide the fate of several members of the Ac-Ac U. faculty. Promotion is perhaps the most important step in anyone's life. I am sure you all remember going through it. A grueling but exhilarating process. It means that the colleagues we endorse with a positive vote here will be with us, hopefully, until their dying day. And our positive vote will lead them down the path to that event that singles out Ac-Ac U., the Induction Ceremony."

What a prospect I thought to myself! To be forever surrounded by the "distinguished" faculty of Ac-Ac U.!

"What are we to look for when making this important decision? Three words that sum up the Ac-Ac U. faculty. Distinction. Distinction. Distinction."

Why should I have been surprised? Had I ever seen this word so abused in my academic life before? Had it not crossed my own mind but a few seconds before? I was frightening myself. Was I beginning to think like the old-timers here? If so, it was a definite sign that I should seriously think of departing this academic asylum.

"Shall we start with a straw vote on Blookoe, our first candidate?"

Gloopersnort got up and headed for the closet behind him. He pulled out a box. An old metal cigar box. Not too "distinguished," I thought to myself. He lovingly carried the box, remained standing, and opened it as he approached the table. My curiosity was getting the better of me. Then Gloopersnort proceeded to do the service, passing the box in front of the various committee members. Was he giving them communion? Each member reverently looked into the box and placed his right hand in it. What would a left-handed individual do here, I wondered? Ac-Ac U. seems to have screened for these abnormalities! The hand disappeared for a few seconds only to resurface as a closed fist. The fist then found its way to the table as if it were self-propelled and sat there.

I was a neutral observer. The contents of the box were still a mystery to me. My eyes were riveted on the fists. Gradually, the table was lined up with clenched fists. All sitting in a row.

"It is time, gentlemen," snorted Gloopersnort, "Alawart Blookoe."

Clank. Clank. Clank. The fists seemed to open all at once. And in an equally speedy motion, they all disappeared under the table. And, there, populating the table were poker chips. All in a row. Green ones. Red ones. Yellow ones. Poker chips? At a promotion committee meeting? Traffic lights, I wondered? This was becoming more and more strange. I must have looked very confused because Gloopersnort started to look at me with concern.

"Oh. I am so sorry, M/M. I should have explained to you what we are doing here. The green chips signal a yes; the red ones a no; and the yellow ones are for a discussion."

So that was it. Now I understood Gloopersnort's secretive walk around the table. He could not permit members of the committee to guess at how their colleagues were voting. The poker chips were counted. The chips of the first candidate, Blookoe (yes, that was his name), for promotion to a Belly Button Tie seemed to be predominantly green. Lucky bastard (I had not forgotten that they were all men!).

Gloopersnort, as head promoter, was tallying the vote: no one else could be trusted to do it. Then he lovingly replaced the chips in the box and off he went. First came the name of the candidate, followed by the ceremonial walk. Around and around, again and again. Offering the box to his committee members, much as a host might lovingly offer delectables to a guest. Definitely an important ceremony, I concluded. Other candidates were not as fortunate as Blookoe, the mostly green promotee. The discussion would undoubtedly be enlightening.

"Well, gentlemen, the results of the straw vote are in. But, as you all know, we cannot simply promote on that basis. The measuring ceremony is perhaps as important as the initial vote."

Gloopersnort lifted his body from his chair and headed for a desk drawer. From it he pulled a tape measure. The tape measure must have been made to order. Red, green, and yellow: alternate stripes in colors to match the poker chips. Was this a prank, I wondered? What the hell were they going to measure? Certainly not their sexual organs. At least, not while I was in the room.

Not to worry. Our fearless leader headed with his tape measure toward piles of dossiers sitting innocently on a table. Their rest was soon to be disturbed, however. Gloopersnort proceeded to measure each pile with his tape measure. Just as lovingly and respectfully as he had performed the poker ceremony. This time, however, he had a helper. The Groin Tie sitting directly to his right. I had noticed this creature when I walked into the room. He had already settled in and seated himself so comfortably that I thought he was part of the furniture. Bald head bent so low that it seemed to be one with the table: much the same color and both shiny. But no. The head slowly moved up from its reading position. This was clearly a human. The thick glasses told it all. He had peered at me without really seeing me and then had simply returned to his work, whatever that was.

As Gloopersnort moved to perform the measuring ceremony, this Groin Tie puffed himself up and raised his head. Obviously, a role he had fulfilled before. His body pulled itself apart from the chair it had been so comfortably glued to. Slowly. Slowly. He worked his way like a worm to a standing position next to Gloopersnort. This creature held in one hand a pen and in the other a notebook with the Ac-Ac U. logo emblazoned proudly on it. How could anyone miss the shiny pink turkey on the green background?

Then began the holy of holies. Gloopersnort standing next to a dossier with his side-kick beside him. Arms outstretched, our noble dean would pull the tape measure from the top of a promotee's dossier to its bottom.

"Blookoe. Twelve inches!" Gloopersnort's voice was booming.

It was as if this voice triggered a rush of excitement. My esteemed male colleagues were inhaling their breaths in one motion, with a giant intake.

"Heh . . . . ." was all I heard.

All this while the Groin Tie side-kick was madly trying to register the number of inches.

The dossiers were measured one by one. There was one two-incher in there somewhere who was clearly a great cause of embarrassment.

As this measuring was done, I could not help but wonder. What about different print styles? Could not one sheet of paper hold half the words of another, more tightly packed sheet?

It was as though Gloopersnort had read my mind.

"For the sake of our distinguished visitor, let me say that Professor Glasshead, my assistant in this measuring process, is the only member of the Ad-Hoc Committee for Equal Publications. This is a life-time appointment. How else can we guarantee continuity? How else can we maintain our distinguished standards? Professor Glasshead has spent literally nights in this office counting the words on the pages of our candidates' publications. He has assured me that this year, for perhaps the first time in Ac-Ac U. history, there is uniformity in the sizes of the pages. Inches of one dossier are the same as inches of another dossier.

"And you know, M/M, our life has not always been so easy. Different size print has been the curse of our promotion process at Ac-Ac U. I am very proud of one thing that I have made sure to instill in every promotion committee with which I have been privileged to work. It is really so simple, M/M, that I am shocked no one has done it before me."

I must have looked very curious. Because before I knew it, Gloopersnort was booming once again.

"Reverse the old adage! Yes. That is what I advise my promotion committees. Reverse the old adage! Never judge a book by its cover is the reverse of what we do here. We certainly judge books by their covers. Important questions are asked: Does a book have a dust jacket? Is the paper shiny? Is there an illustration on the cover or is it merely composed of words? Are there blurbs on the back cover? Is the picture of the author on the back cover? You see, M/M, this is not a simple process for us. Innovate! That is what I encourage my committees to do. Innovate!"

Gloopersnort had finished his speech, along with the measuring process. Gloopersnort and Side-Kick proceeded to sit down. Time for fun. The discussion. I had waited in anticipation for this part of the promotion process. Would the deliberations be identical to the ones I had seen at Pholly U.?

Side-Kick, much to my surprise, was handing out a list of the measures. He had carefully and lovingly copied the figures in a number equivalent to the members of the committee. I was considered one of the privileged few. I received my own copy.

My eyes were moving down the page. There were not too many measurements out of line. Aside from the twelve-incher, most promotees, be it to Belly Button or to Groin status, were middle of the liners. Hovering somewhere between four and seven inches. And then there was that two-incher. What would the committee do?

Gloopersnort kept looking at his watch. I wondered if he had another appointment. Or maybe wifey was expecting him home a bit earlier today. No matter. He was beginning to speak:

"My dear friends. I am pleased and touched by the high quality of the promotees whose dossiers grace our presence this afternoon."

Was he kidding? This made me wonder about earlier promotions.

"Yes. My dear friends. We are indeed blessed. I anticipate that our deliberations will come to an end quickly."

Ah hah! He did have an appointment. I was convinced of that now.

"The straw vote was telling. And the measurements convince me even more. We might have a year of unanimous success."

Gloopersnort was looking at his committee members as he spoke. Some looked a bit confused. I was sure it was the two-incher that was bothering them. They were most likely asking themselves, as was I, whether Gloopersnort had forgotten about him. I wondered if any of them would have the courage to speak up. Side-Kick had reburied his head in the table, the shine of his skull merging once again with that of the wood.

This dean had appointed his committee well. Not one of its members dared to speak up. Gone was the lively interchange of the earlier hour.

"I can tell, dear friends, that some of you are confused. Let us run down the list."

And run he did. Gloopersnort would recite the name of the candidate, followed by two vital statistics: the number of green chips and the number of inches. Gloopersnort knew his statistics. All the candidates were approved for promotion. All but the two-incher. Our noble leader had kept his name for last.

"I see, my good friends, that we are all in substantial agreement. But what are we to do with poor Brunley Arbunkle?"

Brunley Arbunkle was the proud owner of the two-inch dossier. His promotion was to Belly Button.

"Do any of you know Professor Arbunkle personally?" Gloopersnort was not one to give up easily.

An aging Groin Tie at the end of the table spoke up. He had had the privilege of working with Professor Brunley Arbunkle in the Language Application Center.

Like the other committee members, I listened to this Groin Tie fighting for his candidate. But LAC? I had trouble believing it. From DULL to LAC! No one seemed to have noticed the acronym. Just as well, probably.

"Gentlemen."

(*I was about to scream at the fossil. But he was almost in tears.*)

"Gentlemen,"

(*not again, you old fart!*)

"permit me to speak about my good colleague Brunley Arbunkle. What a wonderful specimen of academic integrity! Some have had the bad taste to speak ill of this marvel of intellect that is Professor Arbunkle. How often have I heard those vile tongues arguing that it was his good fortune that his family had the good sense to have their name begin with the first letter of the alphabet, since this would be the only way he could rise to the top of any list. Some have even insinuated that his first name, Brunley, was aptly chosen. After all, if any of us reversed his first and last names, would he not still be at the beginning of the alphabet? No, my good friends. These are not the ABC's of Brunley Arbunkle's world. I dare say that his alphabetical placement has not gone to his head. He is the soul of modesty. If I may add some personal insights, Dean Gloopersnort."

Gloopersnort merely nodded.

"Arbunkle's wife ran off with a student, and a younger one at that. Shameful. This happened not too long ago. This amoral woman left him with two teen-age children to support. That is why, dear friends, I always warn our distinguished faculty members about keeping their students away from their wives. This does not mean that we cannot invite our students to our homes. We simply need to make sure that our wives are not included in the social activities. Is it a wonder that poor Brunley took up with a female underling in his department?"

(A female underling? I wondered what the hell that was. This monologue was really getting on my nerves.)

"Poor man. He needed some emotional support. Those who whisper in the corridors that Brunley changed his clothing, lost weight, and started flexing his muscles are just jealous. Those of us who have had the good fortune to work with Professor Arbunkle know that he is as far from a Don Juan as anyone can be. Ludicrous! The entire thing is ludicrous! Imagine saying that after what happened to him with his wife. Even more ludicrous! I have also been told that after months of this buoyancy he started returning to his old self and gained some of his weight back. The jealous have no limits.

"Trust me, Dean Gloopersnort, I have shut my ears to those who persist in telling me that this small experience in rejuvenation, this sip from the fountain of youth has had a permanent effect on Professor Arbunkle. Far from it. Mind you, I have only noticed that his mind is always on his work. Strutting the hallways! Can you imagine anyone having the indiscretion to speak of a respected colleague in this way? I need not tell you how stunned I was when I then heard from more indiscreet mouths that the new-found love began to have flutterings and hesitations. She was supposedly jealous of some young blond long-haired student. Can you imagine? Have you heard of anything so absurd in your life?"

I was thinking to myself that this Groin Tie was certainly doing an excellent job of massacring his candidate. Not a word about his intellectual endeavors. This was to say nothing of the illegality of the entire endeavor. Mixing Arbunkle's personal life with his professional one. Gloopersnort seemed to be asleep. Is that why he did not interrupt this esteemed Groin Tie when he was going on and on?

"As for Arbunkle's work, dear colleagues,"

Hah! I was not to be disappointed . . .

"That is another story. What a brilliant career that man had ahead of him! What a book he had inside him! But the death of his marriage was a traumatic incident. I fear that his book died with the marriage."

Gloopersnort moved uncomfortably.

"Thank you so much, Professor Nosethump, for this most eloquent defense of a most esteemed colleague. I agree with you that gossip is insidious. We, of course, are in closed session here and the confidentiality of the proceedings is primary. So you need not fear our releasing any of these unsavory details."

Nosethump. I began to remember that I had heard about him from P.H. Gilbert Nosethump. One of the upholders of the LAC program. His specialty? The OP. The OP? I had asked P.H. Yes. The Overhead Projector. Ah! The glory of the intellectual enterprise! The mysteries of the academic universe are indeed multiple and manifold. Nosethump had earned his fame with his revolutionary ideas on one hundred new ways to utilize the OP. I was sure P.H. would be the first to tell me how fortunate I was to be participating in this committee and watching Nosethump in action. In his younger days, apparently, Nosethump had traveled the world spreading the good news about the OP.

"Just think, M/M," I was hearing P.H. saying to me, "every time Gilbert Nosethump's name appears in lights with one of his new theories, the name of Ac-Ac U. is right there with him. What an honor! It almost brings tears to my eyes."

P.H.'s almost tears brought me back to Dean Gloopersnort and his noble gathering. Nosethump clearly had other talents, completely independent of the OP. He had reduced the dean's gathering almost to tears.

"I can tell from the reaction of the audience that Professor Brunley Arbunkle's case is a special one. I do not know him personally. But, as you are all aware, my trust in Professor Nosethump is unwavering. On my own authority, I will promote Professor Arbunkle to the rank of Belly Button Professor."

Sighs of relief surrounded me. My own mind was racing back to Pholly U. There, also, the dean promoted candidates on his say so. And the candidates quickly learned of this administrator's act of selfless and extraordinary generosity. I preferred to think of the Pholly U. dean as a master vampire who would put his academic fangs into the hapless candidates' necks, turning them into his eternal slaves. They could not function without him. But these were not just any victims. They were chosen with care: they had to be of the male gender. For my friends who might find this gruesome metaphor too lugubrious and distasteful, I had created a better one. The dean gave these male candidates life, for without him, they would have been doomed to everlasting unemployment. As for the hapless female candidates? If you are hapless, my dear, you alone are to blame! Such vampires avoid female blood!

Dean Gloopersnort looked calm and at ease as he performed his academic act of life-giving. He had obviously done it before. As for the unfortunate Arbunkle, he would not be the last to enter the hallowed grounds of tenure with but two inches of perorations to his name. I had long been convinced that the inhabitants of academia should be grateful and praise their less gifted colleagues who were incapable of producing anything. After all, do not our eyes also deserve a vacation? Why must we subject them to reading total nonsense? Arbunkle would now bask, as have others before him, in the glory and security of Ac-Ac U. I was, in my own way, hoping that Nosethump was right. That this unwritten book was indeed dead. For some books, I knew, it was better to be dead than read.

Arbunkle may have been by virtue of his name the first on every alphabetical list. Here, he was last. His accession signaled the end of the committee meeting. Gloopersnort had not ceased glancing at his watch. Now he literally ran out of the room. How lucky I was to have S. P.-T. waiting for me! I also ran out of the room, with a mad desire to get to my Guest House and tell all to my friend and companion. P.H. did not care to speak to me nor I to him. Just as well.

In Which M/M Attends the Chairs' Meeting

I would never have guessed that the end of the Promotion Committee meeting would signal the birth of another series of meetings: departmental meetings, chairs' meetings, meetings of the promotees. My mailbox was swamped. It had been fed so many notices that it had begun to regurgitate them. As I walked into the DULL offices, I spotted my mailbox spitting notices at me. A privileged guest had the right to all the privileged university information. Hardly a meeting went by without my receiving a notice about it. Despite my reluctance (I was worried about recording my adventures at Ac-Ac U. for posterity), I had been recycling these wonderful products of the academic thinking machine.

One notice stood out. A meeting for chairs of departments. Hosted by Gloopersnort. In his private seminar room. How could I miss such an opportunity? I gaily made my way once more to Gloopersnort's suite of private offices. What a crowd! There they were. The department chairs. Standing at attention. Awaiting the arrival of the dean. In all shapes and stripes. Some balding. Some not. Some with gray hair. Some not. Some Groin Ties. Some Belly Button Ties. But all dressed to kill. An important occasion.

My arrival raised a few eyebrows. I was sure that all had already heard about me. The oddity of the university. They were whispering among themselves. I could not put a name on any of them. Assam did not seem to be there yet.

Suddenly, there was silence. Gloopersnort was coming around the corner. Mouth grinning, arm waving, he arrived in our midst. I could see that his appointees were appropriately servile. They uttered not a word. He motioned them into the seminar room that had earlier held that other distinguished company, the Promotion Committee. As the assembled group anxiously seated themselves, Assam walked in. Unlike the others who seemed a bit shy, he headed directly for the chair at the dean's right hand.

Strategic move, I thought to myself.

I sat on the left side of Dean Gloopersnort, between two Groin Ties, in one of the few available seats. It only took me seconds to realize why that seat had remained empty. Between them, my two neighbors emitted quite a stench. I had trouble deciding which was the more powerful of the two. Pungent body odor combined with bad breath that reminded me of some other time and place, in which I sat on crowded buses in a foreign country, trying not to vomit. I had then gotten into the habit of carrying little vials of perfume that I would stuff into my nose. This was obviously not part of the etiquette in deans' meetings. I could move my face neither to the left nor to the right. I was surrounded. Either the two fossils were so involved with their work that they had forgotten to wash (the more generous interpretation) or they were simply pigs (the more likely and less generous interpretation).

Gloopersnort was watching me. Did he know what I was going through? I thought I detected a smile on his face. There was an empty seat on his left. Directly across from Assam.

"Well, M/M, since you are our distinguished guest, I would be honored to have you come and sit next to me."

Could I have moved faster? I doubted it. I was impressed, I must admit, by the ease with which Gloopersnort accomplished this. Now I could relax and pay attention to the proceedings rather than having to spend my energies averting my nose from my neighbors.

No agenda was given out for the meeting. Gloopersnort welcomed everyone and announced that, precisely, there was nothing pressing to be announced. I was tempted to respond. Why waste our time? But this was clearly a ceremonial occasion. How many meetings had I chaired at Pholly U. at which business was conducted in five minutes? Yet to dismiss the meeting and not waste the entire hour was so distasteful to some of the committee members that I found myself twiddling my thumbs, listening to the males preach, counting the minutes as they went by.

I decided to watch Assam. Not only was he the only one I knew well but, let us not forget, he was also my chair. He sat with a permanent smile plastered on his face. He could not read everyone's lips at once so he had obviously decided to concentrate his energies on the dean. That certainly made life easier. Whatever Gloopersnort said was clearly of great import. There was Assam nodding gravely just at the right moments. There was Assam smiling at the others. I did not even ask myself if he would vote with the dean on the issues. I knew that he would. A loyal servant, indeed, was my chair.

Gloopersnort was informing his chairs of recent university activities. Who had been promoted. Who had not. The outlook on the budget. No questions were asked. No discussion emerged. Gloopersnort was his usual autocratic self and even my smelly ex-neighbors went along.

This meeting did me in. No interesting individuals. No unusual ceremonies. Just the humdrum activity of an academic meeting. Like many I had seen at Pholly U.

In Which M/M Makes an Important Decision

I arrived at the Guest House completely exhausted. Ac-Ac U. was definitely getting on my nerves. Committee meetings that had no purpose. Pretentious male faculty with nothing to say. Even P.H. seemed to have lost some of his mystery for me. He was present on almost every committee. I could not make an academic step without having him there behind me. Or was it in front of me?

"Well, S. P.-T., what do you think about the idea of going home soon?"

My little darling seemed to really like my idea. She jumped on my lap and started to purr.

"We have had some good times, though, haven't we?"

S. P.-T. was looking at me. Was she remembering, as I was, the incident with the *Festschrift* litter? Just thinking about it made me laugh. I went to pour myself a glass of wine. The decision was effectively made. I would depart from Ac-Ac U. after the next big meeting. A sort of "one meeting for the road." What that meeting would be I still had no idea. But I was hoping it would be a good one.

In Which M/M Has Her Dream Come True

Life was too good to be true. There I was Monday morning in the DULL departmental offices. My mailbox was spitting at me as usual. What should it announce to me this time but a meeting with the provost and his Executive Committee! A special affair. He had heard so much about me. Blah. Blah. Blah. How I would honor him with my visit. Blah. Blah. Blah. How very much his Executive Committee would like to meet with me to discuss questions relating to the essence of Ac-Ac U. The Blah Blah Blah was becoming more and more intriguing as I went along. What a grand ending to my stay at Ac-Ac U. More than I could have wished for. Issues that go to the heart of Ac-Ac U., huh?

Even S. P.-T. was curious. She came over and started sniffing the memo. Then she started to chew on it. Definitely more interesting than anything she and I had encountered yet on this visit.

The meeting with the provost and his committee was not scheduled soon enough for me. On Friday. My departure I decided would be on Saturday. What could I possibly do between Monday and Friday?

In Which M/M Attends an Oral Examination in LAC

I must have been looking quite confused. Because suddenly the rotund figure of Thurber Flysmudge was there beside me.

"Bzzzzzz . . . Ah! Hah! Caught you."

Playing fly was not what I had in mind. Flysmudge was entertaining himself well enough. So why should I respond at all?

"Well, M/M. You look quite bored. What have you got planned today?"

"Actually, not a great deal. I had some things to write up. Why? What do you have in mind?"

"I am on a doctoral committee in the Language Application Center. I am sure you are by now familiar with our extremely distinguished Center."

"You mean LAC?"

"Oh, dear. Oh, dear. I am going to let you in on a secret, M/M. No one—and I repeat no one—calls it by that name. Much too demeaning for a center with those extraordinary qualities. Really."

I was not going to apologize. I had learned one thing in all my years in academia. The bigger the hype, the smaller the organ. So why not give this one a try?

"A doctoral dissertation? What a great idea, Professor Flysmudge!"

"Shall we buzz along? Ha! Ha!"

Flysmudge was laughing so hard at his own joke that I was sure his ball of a body would start rolling on the DULL floor. And no one can tell what could happen next. I suddenly remembered A's story about this distinguished gentleman. I myself started to laugh. At the brain-dead Flysmudge. How would someone like him perform at a doctoral examination? Certainly worth a laugh or two.

It is nice, I thought to myself, that one can laugh at people and have them think you are laughing with them. For an instant, I felt sorry for Flysmudge. But he seemed satisfied enough with his lot.

So we walked out of the DULL office, the two of us laughing. What a sight it must have been. A roly-poly Groin Tie accompanied by the campus celebrity, both in giggles.

How I wish I could say that my merriment continued through the end of the examination! But I cannot.

Flysmudge and I walked into the LAC lounge. The location of the doctoral examination. A round table greeted us. With Flysmudge, the committee was complete. The chair? I recognized him from the Promotion Committee: Gilbert Nosethump. Of Overhead Projector fame. He recognized me as well and welcomed me heartily. A third member was introduced. This was my lucky day. Who should it be but Brunley Arbunkle! Brunley Arbunkle dutifully shook my hand but I could see that his heart was not in the job. Was he thinking about his ex-wife and her new student lover? Or was he thinking about the "female underling," as Nosethump had described her? Or, best of all, was he thinking about his promotion? With his two-inch dossier, he would certainly have much to think about. The promotion announcements had not officially been made yet. Ah! The cruelty of the system!

Someone had thoughtfully placed a bowl of candy on the round table. The center secretary? Or the student trying to sweeten up the committee by getting them high on sugar? The student was not there yet. He would be ushered in after the committee had had a chance to have its strategic powwow. Who would be the first to ask a question? The chair? The brain-dead committee member? Or the obviously preoccupied committee member? I was sure they were going to flip for it. But, no. Democracy was at work. Nosethump would be first.

With this, the student was ushered in. Admit it, M/M, you were surprised. Yes, I admit it, I was surprised. Obviously a foreign student, looking quite ill at ease.

The candidate sat down in the only empty chair and off we went. As introductions were being made, I remembered that LAC was closely associated with DULL. The faculty overlapped between the two. Many foreign students registered in LAC with some doubling in DULL. This was clearly one such case.

"Can you tell us the difference between a thesaurus and a dictionary?"

Nosethump's voice dominated the room.

I was not sure I was hearing Nosethump right. Was this the level at this "distinguished" university? I expected the student to laugh it off and delve into a quick answer. He was silent. I watched him to see whether he knew the answer but thought the question too stupid or whether he simply had no idea. Difficult to tell. After a few minutes of embarrassed silence, I realized that the student had no idea of the difference. He was stumped. He was actually stumped.

Poor Nosethump. He was obviously at a loss. Kind-hearted that he was, he decided to throw another question at this hapless candidate.

"If you had to look up a lollipop in a thesaurus, what would you find?"

"Hmm. Hmm. A lollipop? Well. I would look it up . . . Hmm. A lollipop?"

"Yes. A lollipop. How would one find it in a thesaurus?"

The poor student. His face began to change colors. A great dilemma.

The procedure was driving me crazy. The candy bowl was sitting there. I began to dip into it. My mind began to wander. How odd that the professor should choose a lollipop. Was this the power of suggestion from the candy staring him in the face? If the student had placed the bowl there, then he had written his own funeral oration. Pholly U. was looking more and more appealing as the examination was proceeding. How unfortunate for me that my Ac-Ac U. consciousness should only return after the lollipop question was solved. The student would most likely never forget either the thesaurus or the lollipop.

As for the OP, Nosethump was certainly an active advocate of this most worthy machine. His performance in Gloopersnort's office was no exception for this Groin Tie, I came to learn. From lollipop to OP. That was the next topic. But rather than question the student, there he was preaching the virtues of the Overhead Projector. The student's response? Great relief. His facial muscles actually looked like they might relax sometime in the not-too-distant future.

Flysmudge? His brain was indeed dead. He just smiled and smiled. A nice change from Arbunkle's permanent scowl. I could see that they would be the committee members of choice for any student, be he (for I would discover they were all males) in LAC or DULL.

A bit more on the OP and then there was silence. The student was ushered out of the room for the discussion and ensuing vote. Surprise of surprises. The victim would be saved. His skills? They remained unspecified.

It was Nosethump, oddly enough, who was the student's greatest supporter. He defended him as he might one of his OPs. The bottom line?

"I do believe that this student was simply outstanding. True, the lollipop had him licked. Ha! Ha!"

Nosethump was another one who loved his own plays on words. Flysmudge moved from smile to laughter. Arbunkle had no response.

"What I particularly liked," Nosethump was continuing, "was his analysis of the OP. Outstanding. Simply outstanding."

I looked to Flysmudge and Arbunkle. Had they been conscious enough to realize that there had been no discussion of the OP? That that entire section of the examination was a soliloquy by our team leader? No matter. With any luck, this student would in a few years become a budding young professor at Ac-Ac U. And then nothing could stop him. He was destined, I was sure, for a Groin Tie down the line.

A unanimous decision. Nosethump ceremoniously led the student back into the room and congratulated him on his fine performance. We could all look forward to a fine piece of work, he was sure.

I decided to start looking forward to something else. The end of my stay at Ac-Ac U.

In Which M/M Learns about Ac-Ac U.'S Provost

I had trouble waiting for Friday. After Monday's horrific experience with the LAC doctoral committee during which I thought I would die from an overdose of sugar, I decided to refuse any more official meetings until the one with the provost and his committee. My week was spent clearing the massive amounts of paper I had accumulated in the Guest House.

P.H. had, however, insisted on meeting me and briefing me in advance of the historic meeting. I had to know after all who the provost was, didn't I?

Professor Arosto C. Flubber, holder of the Timeless and Lifetime Chair and a long-standing Groin Tie in the Department of Past, Present, and Future Events. P.H. simply had to furnish me with the story of his meteoric rise at Ac-Ac U.

Flub, as P.H. affectionately called him, had been a non-descript young man on his arrival at Ac-Ac U. decades ago. His dress was undistinguished. His first book, *Hiking and Boating in the Days of the Puritans*, appeared with Pitter Patter University Press. Flub was interested in travel and leisure. But he was trained in the wrong discipline. So he made the best of things and combined his intellectual training with his one passion in life. And this is what gave birth to his first book.

"What a young man Flub was, M/M! I have always been proud of him. His learning skills are beyond compare."

From the story, I could see that Flubber certainly had tremendous learning abilities. When he first arrived at Ac-Ac U., his clothing left much to be desired: striped polyester pants with patterned cotton shirts, the entirety topped by a red wool jacket.

"You know me, M/M. I am not one to judge from externals. But poor Flub was far from manly looking. And his scrawny beard com-

bined with his outdated glasses did not assure him a bright future at
our distinguished institution."

But Flubber's guardian angel was around the corner. Someone
(P.H. would not name this person—I wondered if it might be P.H. himself) high up in the administration took Flubber aside and suggested
that he might wish to join a gym and work out a bit. Then, he should
consider changing his clothing to match his new physique.

As quickly as if he were under the influence of a magic wand in
a fairy tale, Flubber did as he was told. He also shaved off the beard
and threw out the glasses. His vision, it turned out, was not so bad
after all. Besides, was it really necessary for him to see everything so
well? Poof! A new Flubber was born. He was a regular feature in the
university gym. Flexing his muscles alongside those of the upper
strata of Ac-Ac U.'s administration. Laughing along with the high
muckedy muck-mucks. They patted his muscular back. They com-
mented on his new clothing.

Such behavior could hardly go unrewarded. In closed session, at
which P.H. was also present, a secret and highly placed committee
decided to award Arosto C. Flubber the Timeless and Lifetime Chair,
the most distinguished honor that could be bestowed on any faculty
member at Ac-Ac U. Did I detect a tinge of jealousy in P.H.'s voice?
Why not? After all, he was human. It was clear he would never accede
to that level.

Now, nothing could stop Flubber. I remembered reading about
his activities in the newsletter of the Department of Past, Present, and
Future Events. His picture graced almost every page of the newsletter.
One minute he is standing with the president of the university.
Another minute he is in his office surrounded by students working on
his projects. His activities filled the columns of verbiage in the newsletter. He reminded me of a colleague in my own department at Pholly
U., like an amoeba who ate everything in its path. These two were kin-
dred souls. Their projects always took precedence. They mobilized
everyone around them: staff, faculty, and students.

Obviously, Flubber was trying to mobilize me. Make me part of
his entourage. How lucky could I get during my last week at Ac-Ac U.!

In Which M/M Delivers Her Final Blow

Friday. A beautiful day. S. P.-T. woke me up early. She climbed on the bed and started to purr. Demanding that I stroke her.

"You don't have to demand, little one. You know I love doing that."

I sensed her feeling the excitement of the day, our last full day at Ac-Ac U. She was as anxious to depart this place as I was. Was she looking forward to Pholly U.? I doubted it. But, at least, that was home. She could return to her big house and to her birds and squirrels. After all, she had had no friends here whatsoever.

"You know, little one, I find myself in an odd way looking forward to Pholly U. But remind me once I am there not to give up the fight."

Did I detect that knowing smile on S. P.-T.'s face? She knew me better than I knew myself. Me, M/M, give up the fight? My poor chair would literally die laughing if he were to hear it.

Invigorated by the thought of a last committee meeting at Ac-Ac U., I made my way to the provost's office. I sauntered through the campus watching those eager student faces. Professors-ès-Groin crossed my path. Belly Button Professors greeted me. P.H. had volunteered to accompany me to the provost's office. But I had refused. I would simply meet him there. I had not yet informed P.H. of my departure. Which was just as well. I feared that he would insist on my staying and we would simply get into an unpleasant verbal match, not unlike that I had had with him over the meeting with the women faculty.

I headed for the quarters in which the office of the provost was located. Thick, plush rugs greeted me even before I entered the sacred enclosure. I had to traverse banks of secretaries. I heard "May I help you?" so many times with the same syrupy sweet female voice that I thought I would scream.

Finally, I made it. I am not sure what I should describe first. The surroundings or the male individuals inhabiting them.

The plush rugs only got plusher. I was sinking into them. And so was the leather covered furniture: big easy chairs, a sofa. The dark wood paneling on the walls matched the wood desk in one corner of the room. A strong smell greeted my nostrils as I entered the room.

Before I could inquire about it, my eyes focused on three Groin Ties, one of whom was P.H. They all rose to greet me.

"Welcome, M/M. I am Arosto C. Flubber. I am honored and pleased to meet you."

"It is very nice to meet you as well, Provost Flubber."

He beamed. Nothing like those titles to keep them going.

So this was Flubber. He looked like the spitting image of P.H. but younger. More than ever, I was convinced that P.H. was the one who had taken Flub under his wing and guided him on his new path.

Next in line was the Vice President and Dean of Graduate Studies, Midlin Hairline. More of the same meaningless greetings and welcomes. I had heard about him from the women faculty. He stood out in my mind. D had regaled us with one of Midline's more memorable comments. She came to him for something, specifically what is irrelevant. He replied: "If you were a blond, you would get faster service." And there he was, faster-service Hairline. I was fortunate that I could meet most of Ac-Ac U.'s distinguished administrators before my departure.

The smell was getting more pungent. A combination of leather and cigars. It had the distinctive smell of old male power. Oddly enough, no one was smoking. I do not like mysteries.

"That is an interesting smell, Provost Flubber."

"Ah! Yes. We are very proud of ourselves for this. If you will permit me, gentlemen, I will share our secret with M/M."

P.H. and the vice president nodded.

"You see, M/M. I was a student at the Ivies. Don't ask me where. That is not important. I always liked the smell of leather and cigars that one can only be treated to in the exclusive faculty clubs at those institutions. It broke my heart to leave that smell which so reminded me of my youth."

Yes, and of male power, I was about to add.

"So I investigated this problem thoroughly. And lo and behold, I discovered that one can purchase the fragrance. You have no idea how touched I was. It almost brought tears to my eyes. Odor of the Ivies, Xtra Special. That is what it is called. We order it directly from H . . . . . University. We buy it by the box-full. And we spray it in the room before important meetings. It captures the essence of male academia as we knew it and as we would like to remember it."

Inescapable logic. Male academia was what they knew and what they would continue to propagate.

"But, M/M, let us get on to something more pleasurable. I would be honored if you should accept a copy of my most recent work."

With this Flubber handed me a book, *Flubber Flubbers*. I leafed through it quickly and discovered it was a travel account of trips that Flubber had taken to various areas of the globe. My eyes went to the dedication:

To M/M—

Another great traveler. May she learn from Ac-Ac U. as much as I learned from my own trips.

Fondly, Flub.

"Thank you, very much, Provost Flubber. I am most honored. I assure you I will read it as soon as the occasion presents itself."

In fact, let us face it. I was touched by the dedication. That was my academic weak spot. I am not sure I liked to be so closely identified with Flubber. But he had not asked my opinion.

Flubber was going to the wood-paneling behind his desk. Surprise! This was a closet. And what should appear in the closet but vintage champagne. On ice. Surrounding the ice bucket and behind it appeared other types of liquor.

My. My. I had never seen this at Pholly U. But then again I had never been privileged to mix with the upper strata of the administration. Did they have secret caches that they also only shared with friends and special visitors? I was seeing Pholly U. in a different light.

In Which M/M Presents
Her Theory about Ac-Ac

Flubber poured the champagne. We all clinked and sipped.

"Now, I fear, we must mix business with pleasure."

Business? I had no idea what Flubber was talking about. Suddenly, I remembered the invitation. Talking to his Executive Committee about matters concerning the essence of Ac-Ac U.

"As you know, M/M, I am in the Department of Past, Present, and Future Events. For as long as I can remember, the department has had an important working group whose major research was based around the name of the islands that house our distinguished university, Ac-Ac.

"What is the name Ac-Ac? What is its origin? What is its history? How do we translate it? Does it have a relationship to animal sounds?

"You see, M/M, we have been struggling with the derivation of the word. Can you help us?"

Was Flubber serious here? His plea sounded quite desperate.

"I am glad to be of help in any way I can, Provost Flubber."

P.H. and his companion on the couch were beaming. Would this be the solution to all their problems?

"I should first tell you, gentlemen, that this is not my area of research. Nevertheless, I happened to be reading a work of criticism. And there in one of the chapters, the author discussed the Islands of Waq-Waq. Might these be your islands?"

"Undoubtedly, M/M. Please continue." This was Flubber.

The other two were also voicing their excitement and their desire to learn more.

"I believe you have just found our paternity."

I decided to lay it out.

"From what I understand, Waq-Waq are a set of islands whose geographical location was not determined precisely. One tradition has it that these were islands on which women grew on trees."

"What?" This was P.H. "Women growing on trees? Ridiculous! Ludicrous!"

"Absolutely ridiculous," echoed his two friends. "Simply ludicrous!"

"Should I continue, gentlemen?"

I could see that they were of two minds. If they were to let me continue, they would be crediting this theory, which they considered ridiculous. On the other hand, their curiosity was unbounded.

Silence. I decided to break it.

"There is another tradition."

I thought I could see relief on their faces.

"In this tradition, a sailor wandered into the islands of Waq-Waq and discovered much to his shock that the islands were governed by a woman ruler and populated by naked virgins."

"What?" the unanimous male voices responded.

P.H. was waking up faster than the other two.

"A queen ruling over naked virgins? Just where are you getting this nonsense from, M/M? I think I would prefer the first possibility of women growing on trees."

"You see, Professor Hoodwinkle, the women growing on trees are not a simple matter. The women hang from their hair and they yell 'Waq-Waq' when they feel the wind and sun. They do this until their hair tears, at which point they fall and die."

"Why, M/M, this is absolutely gruesome."

"Then you might well prefer the other possibility. This is the way certain geographers imagined the islands that only a few moments ago you were ready to embrace as your paternity."

Yet more silence. I knew that neither option was feasible. I mean, what choices was I giving this provost and his exclusive committee? They were madly searching for their paternity and I had provided them with maternity. Sort of.

Flubber rose. He began to pace.

"You have been speaking about a complex of islands named Waq-Waq. Am I correct, M/M?"

"Yes."

"I really do not see then what this has to do with us. We are Ac-Ac. Ac-Ac! Not Waq-Waq!"

I decided not to fight with Flubber. But there was an idea gnawing at me. Why not throw it at these fossils and see their response? After all, was I not leaving this "distinguished" institution tomorrow?

"I think I understand your reluctance, gentlemen. But if you can have an Ac-Ac U. traditionally populated by men, why can you not have an island populated by women?"

"A most interesting question, M/M. Yes, a most interesting question," Flubber responded.

Certainly an innocuous response. I wondered if this was my signal to depart the provost's sacred grounds.

In Which M/M Announces Her Departure

I was toying with the idea of announcing the end of my stay on this island. How do I do it? Do I tell P.H. and let him announce it? Or do I simply depart as I had arrived? I had, after all, fallen from the sky. Why could I not simply disappear in the same way I had arrived?

As I sat discussing with these three male powers of Ac-Ac U., I decided they would be the first to know.

"May I add one more thing, Provost Flubber?"

He was hesitant. Was I going to come up with another crazy idea? I was sure he had heard about my theory of the ties. He merely nodded.

"I shall be leaving Ac-Ac U. tomorrow."

"What?" once again a unanimous response.

"Yes. It is time for me to depart your august and distinguished institution. I hope that you will believe me when I say that I learned a lot from this visit. I am grateful to all of you."

P.H. just sat there with his mouth open. His visitor was going to disappear. He would no longer be able to take pride in his discovery. But I was sure that I would become a mere figment of their imagination soon enough. A woman full professor? And even worse one who was ready to propagate all these crazy notions. Ties as penises. Islands of women. What would be next?

As the idea sank into their aged minds, I thought I felt the relief that follows any surprising news. Sure, I had been an interesting visitor. But my permanent presence would create an imbalance.

Flubber had to be the official voice.

"May I say, M/M, that is has been a great honor and a privilege to have had you as our distinguished guest. Might I also add that you are now a permanent part of the Ac-Ac U. academic family?"

I could barely contain myself. My wildest dreams could not have conjured this up.

Flubber was continuing.

"This means you can return anytime to Ac-Ac U. A permanent position will be held for you in the Department of Unusual Languages and Literatures."

DULL! I could return to DULL anytime my heart desired! Wow! I was sure I knew what S. P.-T. would say.

"Thank you so much, Provost Flubber. I should also tell you that I could not have landed at a better time. It was my great fortune that Professor Hoodwinkle was there to greet me on behalf of Ac-Ac U."

I could tell that P.H. was very proud. I had thanked him officially. He would undoubtedly go down in the annals of Ac-Ac U. history.

In Which M/M Considers Future Possibilities

As Provost Flubber brought the meeting to an end, P.H. rushed toward me. He was not going to let me off the hook so easily.

"M/M. I must express my shock and dismay. How can you possibly leave us?"

"You do remember, I am sure, Professor Hoodwinkle, that I had a life before I landed here."

"Of course. Of course. But I would be pleased to have you reconsider your decision."

"What would I do here at Ac-Ac U. if I were to remain? Would you offer me a Professorship-ès-Groin?"

"Oh, dear. Oh, dear."

I could tell that the idea took him totally by surprise. I decided to rub it in.

"What would you have me do, here, Professor Hoodwinkle? You may remember also that I am already a full professor at Pholly U."

"Oh, dear. Oh, dear."

I was tempted to ask him if he had turned into a broken record. But his entire body was twitching so badly that I knew he was beyond hope. I watched him as he regained his composure.

"You will be glad to know, M/M, that I discussed this problem at length with President Schmeergang. He is deeply convinced, as I am, that you would work miracles in the Ac-Ac U. administration. He was even willing, in his usual generous way, to open a new position for you as Women's Faculty Advisor."

I cracked up. Laughter took hold of me and I could barely control myself.

"A grandiose baby sitter! Is this what you see successful women as, Professor Hoodwinkle?"

"No. No. You have misunderstood me, M/M. This would be a position of great responsibility. Great responsibility, indeed."

"Yes, I am sure, it would be, Professor Hoodwinkle. But you can also understand why I cannot possibly accept it."

Poor P.H. He looked distraught. Had he promised Schmeergang that he could deliver his new pet on a silver platter? It would not surprise me.

"I see, M/M. I see. Will you go back to Pholly U.?"

"Actually, I have not decided. I will return to my home. I will take the next semester off to do some writing and then I will decide."

In Which M/M Is Not Given an Opportunity to Make a Promise

"Writing, eh?"

P.H. was obviously intrigued. His mouth was twitching.

"What kind of writing will you be doing?"

"Frankly, I am not sure."

"Are you thinking about recording your adventures at Ac-Ac U.?"

Crafty man. I decided to put him on the line.

"Do you think I should?"

"Oh, dear. Oh, dear. What a question!"

I was not certain about where P.H. was heading. I knew him well enough to know that his questions were never innocent.

"Well, what do you think, Professor Hoodwinkle?"

"I can't say, M/M. I am sure that the temptation to describe our distinguished and ideal academic universe might be too much for certain people."

"It does sound like a good idea, Professor Hoodwinkle, I must admit."

Certainly, I was not about to reveal that my collection of Ac-Aciana was unique and that it would provide me with ample material for writing, should I choose to do that.

"I would hope, M/M, that if you do decide to chronicle your days with us, that you will be most discreet and talk in general terms and not in specifics. After all, we do not want to reveal the perfect world of Ac-Ac U. to a wider audience, do we? Out of respect for your mentor, Thornwipple, please keep this experience hidden between us."

Out of respect for Thornwipple? Was this old geezer kidding? I was about to object to this but before I knew it, P.H. had disappeared. I looked around me but he was nowhere to be found.

In Which M/M Hands the Manuscript to S. P.-T.

I returned to the Guest House rather preoccupied. I had not promised P.H. that I would not publish the account of my adventures in this academic haven. At the same time, I must admit that I felt a little sorry for my guide on this incredible journey.

Was I "most discreet" in my account? That is a debatable point. Certainly I had done nothing but describe everything as it really took place. What a dilemma! To expose or not to expose.

There I was on my last night at Ac-Ac U. Sitting in the Guest House sipping a glass of wine. Staring at the pile of goodies that would come back with me to my non-Ac-Acian world. Who would believe me otherwise? S. P.-T. sat contentedly watching me as she is wont to do. My only non-Ac-Acian witness to the events of the past few months. I could tell that she was as anxious to depart as I was.

I suddenly had a mad idea. S. P.-T. How many evenings had she sat listening to me expose to her the madness of Ac-Ac U.? She shared in the adventure. I could not have survived it without her. She knows that only too well. I have narrated the experience. She should publish it.

Afterword

(Post)Landing

Do I believe in fate? I am not sure that I do. But M/M's novel could not have appeared in my professional life at a better time. I was in the midst of plotting a course on feminist utopias and dystopias. The usual list of suspects graced my course: Charlotte Perkins Gilman, Joanna Russ, Katharine Burdekin, Margaret Atwood, Katherine Forrest and so on. (For my absence of footnotes, I invoke a character in Jane Smiley's *Moo*: "Novelists never have to footnote.") The more I read in *Ac-Ac*, the more I decided that M/M's novel was destined for my course.

M/M, the first-person narrator of *Ac-Ac*, is a woman professor from Pholly University who lands on the Islands of Ac-Ac with her feline companion, S. P.-T. The pride of the islands is the academic institution of Ac-Ac U., a male stronghold which has begun to hire women faculty in the past few years. Who should discover M/M as she lands but one of Ac-Ac U.'s senior faculty members, Professor Hoodwinkle? The first professor hired to teach, he, as M/M puts it, "filled the institution (the right word for it!) in his own image." This fortuitous coincidence means that M/M becomes Professor Hoodwinkle's protégé of sorts and she is invited to partake of an elaborate academic smorgasbord that includes various departmental, college, and university affairs. An English professor at Pholly U., M/M spends her period at Ac-Ac U. as an interim member of the university's Department of Unusual Languages and Literatures, otherwise known as DULL. She is the only woman faculty member in that distinguished Ac-Acian department.

This gender distinction is not unique. M/M is also the only woman who appears at the seemingly endless variety of "distinguished" meetings that are the pride of Ac-Ac U. M/M weaves her way through this maze, becoming progressively more disillusioned with these ceremonial occasions. It is only the five junior women faculty who provide a reprieve: she meets them twice, both occasions instigated by her own desires. At the end of the novel, M/M departs Ac-Ac U.

M/M's novel, I was convinced, would help give another dimension to my projected course on feminist utopias and dystopias. Many of the ingredients were there: a female hero who falls from the sky and lands on an island predominantly populated by male academics; a guide who leads the hero through the intricacies of this strange society into which she falls; the hero becomes—albeit for a brief time—a member of this society, only to eventually abandon the dystopian territory. Religious, social, and political issues were already prevalent in the readings I had collected. *Ac-Ac* would add an interesting academic angle.

Yet, what an ironic twist for my students to be asked to look at the universe they were inhabiting from this dystopian perspective! I must admit that when I first delved into M/M's text, I was initially concerned about Ac-Ac U.'s student population. After all, how would my own undergraduate and graduate students react if their Ac-Acian colleagues were savagely satirized? Fortunately, I was to discover, the narrator had almost completely spared students. They are present at the institutions of higher learning, but as part of the background: a student evaluation here, a sexually harassed student there. Absent as major characters, they escape relatively unscathed.

The fact that *Ac-Ac* created a dystopian space did not mean that other literary and narrative characteristics were missing. Humor, satire, powerful imagery: what more could I want in a novel to be digested by both the undergraduate and graduate populations of my own academic institution? If my students did not know the word "distinguished" before reading *Ac-Ac*, they certainly would after reading it: it emanated from the mouths of the male inhabitants of Ac-Ac U. like the air these mouths exhaled.

And, to be honest, there was inherently something that appealed to me on a basic gut level: the fact that the female hero shares this adventure with her female cat, S. P.-T. I myself am a firm believer in the superiority of felines over other creatures (please do not press me on this as it might create unfavorable comparisons with my own species!). And this was clearly no ordinary feline: had she not, after all, received the MacCatArthur Award from M/M? She was listener, voiceless commentator, and much much more, all to be revealed as we weave our way through the maze of an Afterword.

Unlike M/M who lands on the mythical Islands of Ac-Ac, I had landed on a concrete text. But like M/M, whose eventual but temporary integration into the mad world of Ac-Ac comes about in stages, as first she lands on the island, then in a department, and lastly in the University Guest House, so my trajectory had moved first from a brown-wrapped box then to a letter and finally into the strange Ac-Acian universe into which M/M had invited me.

The Guide(s)

Nor once invited, did I feel that M/M abandoned me. She, after all, was well aware I am sure (she is an English professor, let us not forget) that she did not venture into the world of Ac-Ac without a guide, a role admirably played by Professor Hoodwinkle. He is the first male character to speak in the novel.

And what an elderly specimen of Ac-Acian malehood! Well-placed—and well-heeled in Ac-Ac U.'s academic hierarchy—Hoodwinkle facilitates M/M's entry into the male power structure of the university. In fact, it is at his suggestion that M/M decides to become a visiting professor at that respected institution of higher learning, a position that gives her an unparalleled vantage point for her observations and activities.

As for me, therefore, my partial guide was M/M herself. But whereas Hoodwinkle had a solid identity, that of M/M was most unsettled (and unsettling). Her choice was to be either a beginning assistant professor or a ten-year veteran of the academic battlefield. Who wants a naive guide? Ten years of departmental in-fighting at Pholly U. turned M/M into an astute observer of the Ac-Acian dystopian universe. I was pleased to have her settle into the role of experienced full professor as she led me into the hallowed halls of Ac-Ac U.

After all, who but someone of M/M's standing with books to her name could have ensured that the feline character in the novel did not fall victim to the whims of the university's male hierarchy, for whom cats were far from destined to inhabit Ac-Ac U.'s Guest House? The female S. P.-T. proves to be M/M's one faithful companion, the ever-present reminder of the other, non-Ac-Acian, world to which M/M also belongs.

M/M and S. P.-T. are so close that they might as well be one. I know. I know. How can a feline and a human be one? I can answer this natural question in at least two ways: 1) If one can have the Islands of Ac-Ac, why can one not have this union? And 2) (more significantly) have you read any canine mysteries by Susan Conant (or seen the picture on the dust jacket flap of Marjorie Garber's *Dog Love*)? If the answer is no, then I urge you to. If the answer is yes, then I rest my case.

Nevertheless, I feel that I must adduce internal textual arguments for the sake of my own academic reputation. First and foremost, M/M speaks of S. P.-T. and says: "I certainly could not have written my books without her." More importantly, the first-person narrator expresses her and S. P.-T.'s gratitude over the fact that they do not need the DULL mimeographed series to publish "our work." Not only that but M/M admits to being a misanthrope, while arguing that her companion, S. P.-T., loves company. One complements the other.

In fact, S. P.-T. and M/M are such a powerful feline-human combo that *Ac-Ac* would not be the text it is without their joint collaboration. How else do we explain one of the most interesting narrative features of *Ac-Ac*? Here we have a first-person narrator who skillfully and with a great deal of humor entertains the reader. From internal textual evidence, this first-person narrator, not surprisingly, turns out to be M/M. Then there are those elusive chapter headings all of which begin with the ubiquitous three words, "In Which M/M," followed by the activities of the chapter in question. In these chapter titles, M/M is obviously not the first-person narrator, becoming instead a character like the many other characters populating the dystopian territory.

Who is then responsible for these titles that pull the text away from the first-person human narrator? Who but the feline S. P.-T.? Did not M/M after all in her last action in the last chapter hand the manuscript over to her companion and the only witness to corroborate the strange events in this novel? Were not the last words of the human M/M a declaration that she narrated the adventure and that the feline S. P.-T. should publish it?

There are those who will strongly object. After all, they will argue, what about the fact that S. P.-T.'s name also appears in some of the chapter titles? My answer: a subterfuge. Simply, a literary ruse to pull away from the feline influence and to mislead readers.

For you, the doubting reader (I strongly suspect that you are still out there somewhere shaking your head in disbelief despite my evidence), I invite you to reread for yourself how S. P.-T. interacts directly—and quite eloquently—with the intellectual life of the Department of Unusual Languages and Literatures. Only thus can one understand how M/M could award S. P-T. the much-coveted genius prize for felines. How much more lonely would have been M/M's saga had she crashed alone on the Islands of Ac-Ac, without the company of her beloved companion. S. P.-T., I was sure, was there from the beginning guiding me as well through the labyrinths of Ac-Ac U.

Both M/M and S. P.-T., in a sense, are pioneers, going forth into alien territory—and even surviving the adventure well enough to transpose it into words.

The Body

And what a territory! If Ac-Ac had to be defined in one word, it would be the body. More words—yet not too many—will do this def-

inition proud: the university body. The university body in all its rami-
fications is what transforms Ac-Ac U. from being just any university
into an academic institution that is first and foremost a territory of the
body, both as corporal entity and as component of a discourse of sex-
uality.

Male bodies dominate. I hesitate to say that this should not be
surprising, but will say it nevertheless. How could it be otherwise
when the very structure of academic ranks at Ac-Ac U. is intimately
linked to the body? The hallmark of Ac-Ac U. is precisely this link
between university rank and male body: a hallmark already savored
by the reader of *Ac-Ac*. Ac-Ac U.'s professorial titles revolve around
body parts: the Professor-ès-Groin is the senior rank and the Belly Button Professor, the lower one. This is an interesting reverse hierarchy
based on a corporal geography of the human body, where the more
senior rank is farther away from the seat of learning.

But titles are only half the body story. From the deaf chair of
DULL to the brain-dead Professor Thurber Flysmudge, Ac-Ac U.
stands as testimony to the cult of the male academic body, and preferably the older one. The veterans of academia, those who have shared
in its glories, will easily recognize that this is no body beautiful.

Like all readers, however, I have my favorite Ac-Acian male bodies. Who could forget the Professor-ès-Groin at Dean Gloopersnort's
Promotion Committee Meeting? M/M is the one to best describe this
specimen who "seated himself so comfortably that I thought he was
part of the furniture. Bald head bent so low that it seemed to be one
with the table: much the same color and both shiny." As the dean
moves, this "creature" follows suit: "His body pulled itself apart from
the chair it had been so comfortably glued to. Slowly. Slowly. He
worked his way like a worm to a standing position next to Gloopersnort."

The insolence of the first-person narrator as she describes the
male body is at times beyond compare. Reading the depiction of Professor Le Pneu and his male body inflating and deflating with hot air,
even as he is sitting in his chair, I was reminded of one of my own colleagues. As he took the liberty—uninvited, of course—of serving me a
bowl of bile in my office one day, his body seemed to grow inside the
chair it inhabited. His chest filled with air and his face became progressively redder and redder. If I were not convinced that it was cor-
porally impossible, I would have expected his body to burst on the
spot, spilling his bowl of bile—and other things—all over my office (I
limit my imagery here for the sake of the sensitive reader).

The hot air was M/M's touch. I could not help but wonder, however, what the relationship of this hot air in the inflating and deflating male was to the hot air in the balloon that crashes in the first sentence of the novel. I leave the exploration of this relationship—and what it might possibly reveal about M/M's entire project—to critics more astute than I.

Among the male creatures that inhabit Ac-Ac U., perhaps the most provocative are the Ac-Ac-ettes. In their case, the male body acts as the locus for other phantasms that link more directly to a subtext in M/M's novel: the sexual. The university's "Cheering Squad," these Ac-Ac-ettes arrive on the stage during the first faculty meeting. Composed of second-year male assistant professors, this squad demonstrates the complexity of the corporal discourses in *Ac-Ac*. Dressed— or rather cross-dressed—"in shocking pink hot pants" and green sweaters carrying Ac.-Ac. U.'s logo (a shocking pink smiling turkey, face facing outwards with open arms), the ten-member group parades on the stage with batons and pompoms. For God's sake, I wanted to tell myself: batons and pompoms? Batons? Pompoms? Please! Had anyone, I wondered, studied cheer-leading and its languages?

But before I could answer my own question, I remembered that M/M herself spoke about cross-dressing. She admits that she shops in the men's clothing sections of department stores. More intriguing is her confession that she has been known to wear ties. True, she sometimes slings them around her neck like a scarf. Nevertheless, this is a statement that the reader of *Ac-Ac* must reconcile with the narrator's vestimentary theories which she presents to the academic powers at Ac-Ac U.

At the same time, M/M's narration winks at the reader with various sexual innuendoes. She lands on the Islands of Ac-Ac dressed in unisexual clothing and short hair hidden under a hat. It is only when she answers Hoodwinkle's questions about her identity that he exclaims: "A woman." Her voice, not her clothing, seals her gender. Then there is the account of sexual harassment in her home institution, the reference to her own breaking of the code of silence before Ac-Ac U.'s president as an "unnatural act." We could adduce many more (un)savory examples.

As the male body parades itself in and out of the Ac-Acian academic universe, proud and confident, the female body stands in a category of its own. When M/M meets with the five junior women faculty of Ac-Ac U., she talks about how as a "budding young professor," she polished her nails. "But the bright and expensive nail polish could not hide the dirt and bruises that were embedded in my finger nails from clawing my way up in the system." This needs no commentary.

The obsession with the body, clearly, resides both with the narrator and with the dystopian territory in which she is but a temporary visitor.

Scholarship

Lest the reader of my humble contribution accuse me of fiction when I say that Ac-Ac U. is first and foremost a domain of the university body, I take the liberty of citing the title of M/M's thesis: "Reading as a Marxist, Masturbating as a Woman."

Here we have on the first pages of *Ac-Ac* the body, but this time the body set up in a clear nexus with the scholarly enterprise: the act of reading in a given school of criticism and the act of masturbating. Nor is this a literary accident. A disturbing permeability exists between the territory of the body and scholarship. How else can we interpret Professor Schnoozeheit's work in which he measures the size of the human mouth as it opens?

As I pondered my own role of writer of a postduction, I could not help but question the silliness of the scholarly and academic enterprise in Ac-Ac U. M/M's home department of DULL takes pride of place here. A course on sleeping through the ages in which students practice the fine art of losing their waking state?

And this is not to speak of the department's publication series. Hoodwinkle advocates this series to M/M, even suggesting that some of its over nine hundred titles would surely interest her. "Fine masterpieces of literary scholarship," as he describes them. When M/M inquires further, she hears:

> "Oh, yes. The best plot summaries to be found anywhere. Some of our young scholars have dedicated themselves to this enterprise. I will let you in on a secret, M/M. These summaries are better than reading the original. Yes, if I do say so myself. They are wonderful. Absolutely wonderful."

Is it any wonder that this department prides itself on its "No-Think Clause?" Thinking was not part of the faculty's mandates in DULL. In fact, quite the opposite. The administration forbade them to think, and as far as the history of this strange phenomenon, how can we ourselves think about it, if even the DULL faculty members do not (what else could one do with a name like DULL?)? I certainly could not do more justice to the "No-Think Clause" of M/M's home department than to let its jingle speak for itself:

Do not think.
Do not think.
Help to keep us in the pink.
New ideas are oft divisive.
Prima donnas get derisive.
Do not think.

In an odd way, the reader should then not be surprised that the distinguished male academic chosen to receive the Muted Language Society Award, Professor J. P. Snootpile, should be associated with—and congratulated for—a book that earns him the label of "Absent Prose" Snootpile, precisely because ninety-nine percent of his prize-winning text is composed of quotations from other people's work.

Both M/M and her readers discover that scholarship at the "distinguished" institution that is Ac-Ac U. is consistently carried to new heights.

Tradition

The book-award ceremony which M/M is privileged to attend, like the other prestigious events and committee meetings to which she is invited, is a testimony to Ac-Ac U.'s highest academic traditions. M/M hops from one "distinguished" gathering to another, gatherings that are populated by the male elite of the institution intent on maintaining their self-propagating tradition.

As I watched M/M seemingly swimming in this sea of revered male tradition, I became acutely aware of my own assignment with which M/M herself had very unceremoniously and untraditionally saddled me. Rethinking my task, I began questioning the very notion of an afterword. After all, did not a scholarly analysis of a work traditionally require a biography of the author? And where was the author here? For all intents and purposes, M/M had forwarded me the package and disappeared. The only "biographical" data remaining were what she herself, as narrator, chose to reveal to her readers. Need I add that in a work of fiction, this type of data is best set aside? I invite my reader to glance once again at the first chapter of *Ac-Ac*. How reliable, after all, is M/M's "biographical" information if she hesitates at the very outset (the novel's first chapter) about whether she is to be a ten-year academic veteran and a full professor or a beginning "unpredictable" assistant professor?

And as if it were not challenging enough for me as writer of an afterword to have this instability in professorial identity, I was having to face an instability in onomastic identity. What was I to do with the name M/M? Two identical letters with a slash between them. In his first interchange with the female hero, Hoodwinkle asks: "M period M period?" To which M/M replies: "No. M slash M." No other information is forthcoming. As I read and reread this first interchange between Hoodwinkle and M/M, especially in light of the onomastic games in the novel, I realized that M/M's response is a clear act of defiance, with a hint of violence.

Taking my task quite seriously, however, I was not to be deterred. M/M had graciously mentioned that Hoodwinkle had sent "one of his minions to the library to look me up and sure enough my books showed up on the data banks." Not being one to leave my research to others, I imitated the act of Hoodwinkle's assistant. I searched and searched: the computerized catalogues, the older non-computerized catalogues, author listings, title listings, everything conceivable. I had even enlisted the help of my own institution's reference librarian. Nothing. There was no M/M to be found anywhere. If not even the name was there, how was I to find her books? Was Ac-Ac U. blessed by a more comprehensive library than my own research institution? These and other questions remain by necessity unanswered.

The Name

The reference librarian helping me was more surprised by the name "M/M" than I had been. He (for it was a he) repeatedly asked me in disbelief if I were sure of the spelling of the name. Like Hoodwinkle (whom he had not met I should add, not having read the manuscript), he felt more comfortable transposing the name into "M.M." The more I insisted, the more he became frustrated by this search that yielded no results. I realized then that M/M's books (other than the novel, of course) would remain forever hidden in some library collection unavailable to me.

The male librarian's reaction to the name, however, intrigued me. I had been sensing all along that *Ac-Ac* was an onomastic treasure trove. But the vehemence of his reaction eliminated any hesitations I might have had to investigate the novel's name games.

M/M and S. P.-T. enter the literary scene as consonants. The reader never learns what these letters stand for, if anything. But perhaps that is irrelevant. These two appellations must be seen in the larger context of the onomastic project of M/M's novel. In the strange Ac-Acian universe, women are not endowed with names. The female faculty identify themselves for M/M with the letters of the alphabet:

from A to E, basing their onomastic decision on their very "sensitive position at Ac-Ac U."

The issue is infinitely more complicated. The men who inhabit the university are endowed with full-blown names. But their names are complex constructions that lean to the satirical. And many are also pre-destined names of sorts. One example will suffice here: Le Pneu we all know means "tire." What a happy coincidence it should be that he is the Professor-ès-Groin who inflates and deflates with hot air. Ironically enough, it is the brain-dead Flysmudge who seems to be aware of at least some of the games being played with names. As he first meets M/M, he declares: "You are probably wondering about my name. I realize that it is rather unorthodox and believe me I have been subjected to many a joke about it." Professor Flysmudge even played with his own name and had gone so far as to have a plaque inscribed with what was known "lovingly in DULL as the 'No Swat Motto,'" because he would not kill flies. It is as if the other male inhabitants of this strange onomastic universe were completely oblivious to the deeper implications of their names. Perhaps one needs to be brain-dead in this Ac-Acian universe to fully grasp its more preposterous aspects.

I leave my astute reader the pleasure of discovering the other hidden onomastic treasures in M/M's text. An aside here: these name games made me wonder if M/M was what she claimed to be, that is an English professor. Her linguistic arsenal convinced me that she must be more.

In *Ac-Ac*, therefore, complex names, and not ones simply composed of letters, are more often than not the occasion for mockery. In a sense then it is appropriate that the women faculty should have been onomastically restricted to letters of the alphabet and no more. Had they had names, these names would most likely have been constructed comically, becoming potential subjects of the satirical bent of the text. With their initials, the women faculty escape the onomastic ridicule destined for their male colleagues.

This stripped-down onomastics, if I may call it that, gets its full articulation at the first meeting M/M set up with Ac-Ac U.'s women faculty (all five of them!) in her temporary home, the University Guest House. Of course, the women voluntarily choose to occult their names to keep their identities hidden. Is it a literary coincidence that, like the visitor who fell from space, these women academics identify themselves with simple letters? Is this a subtle game of emulation and imitation of M/M whose name throughout the novel is perceived as a challenge to Ac-Ac U.? Or did these women faculty sense that someday they might become characters in a dystopia? Perhaps.

And then again perhaps not. One of the women faculty, A, turns out to be a great storyteller. Let us drop in on the beginning of her first story:

> "Do you remember the time that Flysmudge fainted?"
> "Flysmudge? Of DULL fame?" I responded.
> "Yes."
> We were all giggling. The name itself. I had been struck by it when I first met the great man himself at the DULL reception. But, here, among us women, it seemed even more ridiculous.

In M/M's private quarters, the women form a bond that permits them to view their male colleagues in a different light. Male names that might have simply struck one's fancy in the "normal" world of Ac-Ac U. take on a different signification among the women faculty. Already strange, the names become "even more ridiculous." The gender solidarity of the women as a group permits this transformation to take place (and, of course, all the wine imbibed at M/M's party helps as well!).

Laughter and ridiculousness aside, any critic knows that endowing characters with names is a way of solidifying their identity. The fact that the women faculty, including M/M here, are not full participants in this onomastic process means that their individual identity remains outside the norm of the academic institution in which they are supposedly faculty participants. A deep sense of alienation pervades their academic existence.

M/M understands all this quite well. Her attempt to strip some of the males of their names and reduce them to mere initials is a way for her to reduce their institutional status. Certainly, she performs this exercise with Professor Hoodwinkle, for one, who is gradually turned into P.H. She restrains herself, however, and never addresses him this way directly. Is she afraid, if she were to shorten it in his presence, of breaking the rules of professional decorum to which she adheres? Or is she simply trying to keep him out of the inner circle of characters whose openly stripped-down names are worn like badges of honor in an onomastic system that favors full names and then satirizes them?

Hierarchy

Once again, let us allow M/M to guide us on this thorny path. Early on in the novel, as she is still getting her bearings and deciding on her future at Ac-Ac U., she "Gets a Lecture on Academic Hierarchies."

I could tell that P.H. felt uncomfortable with my name.

"Just M/M, huh?" he would repeatedly and emphatically ask.

"Yes," I would just as repeatedly and just as emphatically answer.

"No Professor or Dr. before it?"

"No."

By now, P.H. had accepted, albeit not too gracefully, my status as full professor at the institution he so much admired. He had also sent one of his minions to the library to look me up and sure enough my books showed up on the data banks. So I was a bona fide person.

But no title? That really seemed to bother him.

"You know, M/M, our fine university thrives on titles. How else would we spot the professors from the mere hangers-on? No institution can exist without hierarchy. What else would our colleagues have to live for if they did not have that?"

Poor P.H. His mouth was twitching. He could barely get the words out.

"I am sorry, *Professor* Hoodwinkle."

I was sure to put the emphasis on Professor.

"M/M it will be."

"As you wish, M/M."

He grudgingly gave in. Not only was I challenging the hierarchy but I was challenging his authority. This test of wills was important for me. He promised me he would make sure his colleagues addressed me as I wished to be addressed.

This detailed interchange between M/M and Hoodwinkle highlights several points. M/M's existence as "a bona fide person" must be established by a library search that turns up her works. But this is not enough for the status-conscious Hoodwinkle. M/M rejects the hierarchy inherent in academic titles, be they Professor or Dr. Her guide, on the other hand, is not happy about this outcome since it threatens the inherent power structure of the dystopia of which he forms a part. For him, a stripped-down name is far from perfect, a title being an essential part of what defines and delimits identity.

Both M/M and the other women academics in *Ac-Ac* reject this hierarchy based on names and titles. And their rejection of this phenomenon must be seen in the larger context of the prevalent male homosocial universe of the novel. In fact, this Ac-Acian universe functions almost as an ode to male homosocial bonding. Ac-Ac U. administrators have different sorts of seemingly friendly physical contact with their male faculty in the various official settings: a pat on someone's back here, an arm around someone else there.

The males appear to be extremely comfortable with the institutional power structure. Their homosocial bonding takes place in an academic and intellectual setting. And this is why scholarship in Ac-Ac U., no matter how ridiculous, is intimately connected to the men. The young women faculty who meet with the alien visitor do not have a scholarly existence. They do not appear to participate in the scholarly enterprise and not a single one speaks to M/M of her research. This is undoubtedly in part due to the fact that men dominate this area in the dystopian universe. But in part we cannot discount the fact that in this way women's research, like their names or the subject of students, is kept at a safe distance from M/M's savage attack.

To counter this seemingly impenetrable male world, the women also form a homosocial unit. But their homosociality differs from that of the men. The women have to do their bonding in a social setting, not in an academic or intellectual one. They meet at the Guest House over wine and cheese, instead of in some exclusive seminar room owned by the dean or the president of the university.

As I pondered this point, I thought of its applicability in the dystopian territories which some of us inhabit daily thanks to our own academic institutions. Does *Ac-Ac* mean to suggest that academic women's apparent gatherings by their nature veer to the social rather than the academic?

This, of course, does not mean that the men of Ac-Ac U. do not partake of the social. But their more social activities, like eating, are defined in terms of a gender hierarchy. M/M will once again guide us, this time through the luncheon ritual.

P.H. had explained to me quite proudly that the wives of the Ac-Ac U. professors were very supportive "good little girls" (read: unlike you, M/M). They made their hubbies' lunch. And what grateful hubbies they were! One could see them munching the sandwiches, savoring every bite in the appropriate university locations. Departmental seminar rooms became dens of crunching mouths at lunch time. It had taken me a while to figure out that when individuals "did lunch" at Ac-Ac U., it meant that each took out his respective sandwich and gobbled it in the company of the other. Each priding himself on the fact that his sandwich was thicker. I wondered: what was the relationship between the

thick sandwich and the length of the tie? Were wives here sublimating their own desires and ambitions into thick sandwiches?

Need I analyze this? I am sparing my reader a discussion of the obviously hierarchical assumptions behind much of Hoodwinkle's discussion of heterosexuality and the value of "wives."

    The complexities of these gender and social hierarchies are well
exemplified by Hungarian Goulash. Professor Kupferhoff of DULL
(what else!) was famous for his Hungarian Goulash, a "savory dish
that made an appearance at every annual departmental picnic." So by
popular demand, Kupferhoff's recipe was provided to the reader in
the DULL Newsletter. This Hungarian Goulash recipe might seem to
initially argue against the notion that it is the women faculty who are
restricted to the non-intellectual domains. But, in fact, the opposite is
the case. By transforming a food item into its printed version, a recipe,
the editors of the DULL Newsletter have assimilated it to the other
materials in the newsletter, and permitted it to enter the domain of the
intellectual. Notice that the newsletter did not provide recipes from the
faculty wives: only the male product merits inclusion in the sphere of
the printed word.

Discourses

    If women in the academic dystopian universe of *Ac-Ac* are not
fully partaking of the hierarchical pleasures and joys of academia,
what are they doing? Superficially, their presence seems to be to challenge the gender assumptions beloved of the top administrators of Ac-
Ac U. This is most obviously the case in the discussions over the possible promotion of women faculty, especially to the rank of
Professor-ès-Groin.

    But, in fact, there is much more to the gender dynamics than first
meets the eye. Women do have their words in the dystopian universe
of *Ac-Ac*, words that are shared in the privacy of M/M's Guest Suite
during the two meetings.

    We need to understand the impact of these women's words
against the background of the two meetings themselves. To say that
M/M had a great deal of difficulty setting up the first meeting with the
Ac-Acian women faculty would be an understatement. The institutional resistance to this gathering was enormous. The vehement interchange between M/M and Hoodwinkle is a case in point. He wishes
to attend "what he calls the 'women's meeting.'" M/M does not wish
him to. It is only when she threatens that she will leave him standing

at the door should he insist on arriving for the meeting that he finally gives up. Then there is disagreement about the location of this gathering. Hoodwinkle reluctantly agrees to M/M's idea that the meeting should take place in the Guest Suite with the statement: "At least in your suite, no one will see you." M/M puts all of this in perspective: "It was as if there were some conspiracy between us to do something illegal."

Why all this anxiety over a meeting of women faculty? Is it simply because they will "exchange ideas" or "share feelings," to quote M/M?

In fact, the anxiety of the Ac-Acian male establishment was not displaced. The women faculty are performing a highly subversive act. In the two meetings, they create a parallel discourse that counters that of the Ac-Acian male "distinguished" discourse.

In her daily meanderings through Ac-Ac U., M/M comes in contact with male academics. Their adventures do nothing but praise the academy. The women faculty provide an unofficial counter-history of the university. As A tells the tales of the brain-dead Flysmudge and the sexual harassment by Kleinputz, the reader is exposed to another narrative, one that makes it clear that all is not what it seems to be in the world of Ac-Ac U. Here we learn how it was that the university discovered that Professor Flysmudge was—and had been—brain-dead and the administrative cover-up that this finding necessitated.

Since the first meeting with the women faculty occurs about half way in the novel, it means that the female discourse is there as a backdrop to the male discourse, countering it and modifying it. Hoodwinkle's fear of the "women's meeting" would appear to have been justified. Imagine if he knew that M/M met with the women faculty a second time and heard even more unexpurgated stories about the lofty institution that was Ac-Ac U.

The counter-discourse established by the women is complex. On the one hand there are the stories told by A who regales her female listeners on both occasions. On the other hand there is the poetry. M/M recites her own poetry in the first meeting. In the second meeting, B joins in. All the poems confirm the existence of the gender hierarchies with which the reader is already familiar.

In the second meeting, B and M/M recite two poems. B's poem addresses the male and female body, whereas that of M/M invokes woman's inability to achieve what a man can. The two poems, recited one after the other, initially seem very far one from the other. But M/M alerts her reader: "I felt that my poem was functioning like an answer to hers. We were moving in the same universe."

This movement speaks to the constancy of gender and sexual politics in that universe that M/M and her female colleagues are populating. The poems function as a commentary to the non-changing face of the academic tradition surrounding these women faculty members. The corporal definition of women (B's poem) and their hierarchical and intellectual positions (M/M's poem) are immutable.

Are B and M/M overly negative in their poetic discourse? Not by any means. At the end of the novel, as M/M announces her departure, she discovers that Ac-Ac U. had great plans for her. She could remain at the institution but not as a Professor-ès-Groin. She could become the Women's Faculty Advisor. Despite her extended stay at Ac-Ac U. and despite her scholarly reputation, she has not succeeded in altering the view of the male establishment: her gender defines her and she can never accede to the rank of the males.

The two poems by B and M/M highlight another important point. B is a junior faculty member. M/M is a seasoned veteran of academia. Yet the two poems communicate and confirm the same verdict about women and gender in the academy. The poetic discourse instills the notion that no matter what the rank, academic and gender politics are everlasting.

The brain-dead Thurber Flysmudge will once again permit us to explore this changeless and seemingly eternal aspect of the academic cosmos, while at the same time linking it to gender. In her story about the brain-dead Flysmudge, A had related that "in the old days, he would come up to newcomers at Ac-Ac U. and buzz like a fly." But then who should come up to M/M one day in the DULL department office and buzz at her but Flysmudge himself?

"The old days" are no longer so old, we discover. They are still very much alive. Nothing it would seem has changed on the unchanging face of academia. Women tell stories that they believe are part of the past but experience will teach them that the past and the present are but one.

Conclusion

The ultimate subversive counter-text is, of course, that of M/M herself. She relates the most incredible of all stories, that of the Islands of Ac-Ac on which she lands.

Her own story left me with more questions than answers. I had crafted my critical contribution around the idea of dystopias. I was unwavering in my opinion that this was indeed a feminist dystopia. But now I began to think that perhaps it was other things as well. It had the elements of a complicated and symbolic academic patricide (after all, does not Hoodwinkle seem to simply evaporate at the end of the novel?). Or was *Ac-Ac* some kind of perverse upside-down female *Bildungsroman* in which the hero is back where she started without any *Bildung* at all? Did my postduction need an introduction?

Deciding to err on the side of caution, I elected to reread my contribution again (I had been reading it along as I wrote it, my usual habit). Imagine my shock when I found the following letter embedded in the conclusion to the afterword. I had no memory of having written this letter. Did my own feline companions compose it and attribute it to me? Were they in collusion with S. P.-T.? After all, were they not also Maine Coons? Here is the letter:

My dearest M/M (by now I understand you would not have it any other way),

As I conclude the "introduction" that you so kindly asked me to write to your novel, I want to thank you for having honored me with this task (I mean it!).

I have, however, taken some liberties. I chose to call the entirety of the project *Hisland*. I somehow know that you admire Charlotte Perkins Gilman as much as I do and that you would hence indulge me in the new title (do you think that Gilman will forgive either or both of us?).

If you read my afterword (as I hope you will), you will discover that I, like you, am an inveterate lover of felines. I would not dream of altering your dedication and acknowledgments to *Ac-Ac*. The acknowledgments tell it all: what better combination of colleagues and the body could the reader want?

Please allow me to express my pleasure at your wise choice of full professorship. Not only did this allow you to go up in the hot air balloon but, more importantly, it permitted you to fall from space. All this strikes me as more appropriate for a jaded narrator than the cruise of a beginning—and one hopes still idealistic—young assistant professor.

As soon as I read your letter, I sensed that you knew me better than I knew myself. How did you guess that I too always feel quite the alien? That I always have the sense that I somehow fell out of space and landed by mistake in the world which I now inhabit? Your repeated references to this notion of falling from on high and being an alien did not go unheeded. That is why I was hoping that you would audit Professor Humbert Linguano's course on "How to Speak to Aliens." What a shame that it was not offered at the time you visited Ac-Ac U. I dare not say perhaps next time!

I hope that your return to Pholly U. was uneventful. May your future landings lead to more narratives.

With admiration.
Your Female Fellow Traveler in Academe.

I could have deleted this "alien" text that apparently fell from cyberspace into my computer. But I decided to leave it. It was symptomatic of this entire enterprise in which I was involved. From the novel that landed in my office to the novel's narrator(s) who landed on the Islands of Ac-Ac, I seemed to be involved in strange landings and in events beyond my control.

To be honest, the more I read the letter to M/M, the more I felt it belonged in my own afterword. My feline companions (for I was convinced now that this composition was their work) wanted me to commune directly with M/M and S. P.-T. They had accompanied me on numerous adventures in my own generic Ac-Ac U. of which I had been a member for countless years. Perhaps they too felt it was time to exorcise these adventures.

—*Fedwa Malti-Douglas*